amped bel

STARSTRUCK DOG WALKERS

Cherry Whytock used to be a country bumpkin but is now struggling to become a glossy girl-about-town. She spends a great deal of time in the local coffee shop, gathering strength for her next retail expedition, but becoming a sophisticated 'townie' is proving to be more difficult than she imagined. Even though she now owns at least a million pairs of high-heeled shoes she still feels happier in her wellies. If anything Lily, her boxer, is more of a glossy girl-about-town as she now has a beautiful pink sparkly collar, which she enjoys showing off to her various boyfriends on the common. (Lily has dumped the wire-haired dachshund that she used to be in love with because he kept stealing her biscuits.)

Also available from Piccadilly Press by Cherry Whytock:
Honeysuckle Lovelace – The Dog Walkers' Club
Honeysuckle Lovelace – Ghosthunters

Angel – Deli Dramas and Dreamy Doormen
Angel – Disasters, Diets and D-cups
Angel – Haggis Horrors and Heavenly Bodies
Angel – Loving, Loathing and Luscious Lunches
Angel – Secrets, Suspicions and Sun-kissed Beaches

Cherry Whytock
Honeysuckle Lovelace

STARSTRUCK DOG WALKERS

PICCADILLY PRESS · LONDON

First published in Great Britain in 2007
by Piccadilly Press Ltd,
5 Castle Road, London NW1 8PR
www.piccadillypress.co.uk

A catalogue record for this book is available from the British Library

ISBN: 978 1 85340 945 5 (trade paperback)

1 3 5 7 9 10 8 6 4 2

Printed in the UK by CPI Bookmarque, Croydon, CR0 4TD
Cover design by Simon Davis
Cover illustration by Cherry Whytock

Chapter One

'What do you think, babes: pink or purple?' asked Rita.

Honeysuckle Lovelace squinted at her mum as Rita stood on the deck of their houseboat waving her paintbrush through the air. The early spring sunshine bounced off the rippling canal water while Honeysuckle considered. 'Pink!' she said finally.

'That's what I thought,' said Rita, sploshing her brush into the pot of pink paint. 'A girl can never have too much pink!'

The redecoration of the Lovelaces' houseboat had happened every spring for as long as Honeysuckle could remember. Rita always waited until Honeysuckle's half-term when she would take a couple of days off from her hair salon, Curl Up and Dye, before beginning the transformation. They had already painted giant flowers and butterflies all over the roof of The Patchwork Snail and now they were beginning work on the deck.

'I thought we might do stripes, just for a change,' Rita said.

'Great,' said Honeysuckle, scooping back her ton and a half of black curly hair before leaning down to begin her first stripe.

'If I do pink over here,' Rita continued, 'and you do orange over there, we should meet in the middle . . . if we're lucky!'

'OK,' said Honeysuckle, grinning at her mum. She didn't know anyone else who had a mum quite like hers. Surely no one else's mum would ever wear crimson cycling shorts, thick green tights and leopard-print ankle boots to repaint their home. No one else's mum knew the words to all of Abba's greatest hits. No one else's mum had different coloured hair at least every other week. And Honeysuckle was certain that no one else's mum had ever tried as hard as hers to give up smoking.

She wondered for the squillionth time why Lenny, her father, had 'gone off into the wild blue yonder', as Rita said, 'and forgotten to come back'. Honeysuckle thought perhaps he was a bit mad for leaving her mum, but as she couldn't remember anything about him and her mother never talked about him, she had no way of knowing for sure. All she was absolutely, completely and positively certain about was that Lenny was a proper Romany and that it must have been from him that she had inherited her fortune-telling powers. She hadn't told Rita she had special powers; Rita never wanted to hear about anything that reminded her of Lenny.

Honeysuckle loved the smell of the paint and the way it slid from her brush on to the wood. As she watched her orange stripe make its way down the deck, her mind wandered happily around all the things she was going to do during half-term.

If Rita had time, they would trawl the charity shops together for additions to their colourful wardrobes, so they might have to get rid of some of the stuff they already had stored in the little blue shed by the side of the canal. There was nowhere to put much inside The Patchwork Snail so the blue shed had become what Rita described as 'the magic wardrobe'. She and Honeysuckle had occasional sorting sessions when they would sort out all the stuff they didn't wear any more and take it back to the charity shops to be sold again.

Honeysuckle felt a bubble of excitement about the prospect of sifting through the second-hand bargains. But she was even more excited about all the bookings that she and her fellow Dog Walkers had lined up for the half-term holiday.

Word had spread around the small town and the Dog Walkers' Club now had fourteen different clients listed in its lollipop-green registration book. Honeysuckle first had her Brilliant Idea for the Dog Walkers' Club when she saw the image of a dog in her tea-leaves. She was absolutely certain that she could predict the future from tea-leaves and often – well, *sometimes* – she got it right! Her talent for tea-leaf reading was one of the things she had inherited from her dad – that and her dark, curly hair and pale blue eyes. Obviously she didn't tell her mum about the sign and it was only when she noticed their neighbour, Mrs Whitely-Grub, with her poodle, Cupid, in the Curl Up and Dye salon that she understood what the tea-leaves were trying to tell her.

As her second orange stripe slithered on towards the opposite end of the deck Honeysuckle smiled to herself. She thought about the adventures that she and Billy, Jaime and Anita had already had since the Dog Walkers' Club began. There had been The Murdered Major and

The Horrible Haunting – who could guess what might happen next . . .

'Oh, blithering jellyfish!' squawked Rita. 'Look what we've done!' Honeysuckle glanced up. Their pink and orange stripes had lined up all right but they were wiggling like worms all across the deck.

Honeysuckle giggled.

'If only this blinking boat would keep still this would never have happened,' sighed Rita as she drummed her fingers on the newly painted roof. 'Oh, Honeybunch! It's at moments like these that a girl really needs a gasper, just one little ciggie . . .?'

'Oh no, Mum, you mustn't,' pleaded Honeysuckle. 'What did the hypnotherapist tell you to do when you wanted to smoke?'

Honeysuckle knew that Rita had high hopes for hypnotherapy. She had already tried chewing gum, fake cigarettes and nicotine patches in her effort to give up the horrible habit. She had been doing really well until Christmas. Then the strain of dumping her boyfriend Sergeant Monmouth over the holiday had sent her hurtling back to the 'filthy filter tips' again.

'Oh,' sighed Rita. 'The therapist told me to hold on to my right wrist with my left hand, close my eyes, count backwards and go to my favourite place in my head. Then I have to imagine myself calm and in control of my cravings.'

'Don't you think you should do that then?' suggested Honeysuckle. 'Go wherever it is and then you'll stop wanting to smoke.'

Rita grasped her wrist, closed her eyes and began breathing deeply. Honeysuckle couldn't imagine anywhere she would rather be than exactly where she was, on The Patchwork Snail. She wondered where her mum would like to be. She watched her swaying slightly with the gentle swell of the canal and her face began to relax.

A voice suddenly called, 'Yoo hoo!' It was coming from the bridge. Rita's blue-mascaraed eyelashes snapped open.

'Hello!' the voice went on. 'What are you two up to?'

'Oh for goodness' sake!' muttered Rita.

'My! Doesn't The Patchwork Snail look divine?' By now both Rita and Honeysuckle could see the owner of the voice. It was Mrs Whitely-Grub. She had her little pinky-white poodle, Cupid, in her arms and together they were peering over the wall at Honeysuckle and Rita. 'So original! Wavy lines all over the deck! What fun!' Mrs Whitely-Grub exclaimed. Cupid gave a squeaky yapping sound, which made the bow on the top of his head wobble.

Rita looked down at the deck of the houseboat and snorted with laughter. Then she threw back her head and laughed and laughed until the tears smudged eye make-up all down her cheeks.

'Did I say something funny?' asked Mrs Whitely-Grub, looking confused.

'No,' said Rita, giggling. 'It's just that it's all gone wrong – they were meant to be straight!'

'But my dear,' said Mrs Whitely-Grub, 'from up here it looks most original – not at all like a mistake. Come and see!'

Rita and Honeysuckle stepped off the boat and ran through their mini garden and up the stone steps to the street, and on to the bridge.

'There!' said Mrs Whitely-Grub, putting Cupid down on the pavement. 'Do you see how exciting it looks?'

Rita and Honeysuckle gazed down.

'Wow,' Honeysuckle gasped. 'It's fab! Look, Mum, if we just join all the wiggles up at the ends, it's going to look awesome!'

Cupid was yapping wildly and jumping up and down in his excitement at seeing Honeysuckle. She leaned down and gave him a hug. If she was honest, he wasn't her absolute favourite of all the dogs that she and her friends walked but, as he was the founder member of the Dog Walkers' Club, she had a special place in her heart for him.

When the yapping had quietened down a little, Mrs Whitely-Grub turned to Honeysuckle and said, 'I was going to ask you whether you might walk my little Cupie for me this afternoon?'

'Of course!' Honeysuckle replied. 'We have three other dogs to walk at two p.m.,' she went on in her most businesslike voice, 'so it would be a great pleasure!'

Chapter Two

Honeysuckle's brilliant plan for the wiggly-striped deck made Rita forget about wanting to smoke. They bounded down the stone steps, across the tiny garden and back on to the houseboat.

'Okey dokey,' said Rita. 'Here we go!' She began deftly joining the writhing lines with a dab of pink paint here and there. Honeysuckle stood on the prow of the boat and made helpful comments and gave directions.

'There!' she said triumphantly. 'It's all done! Come and have a look!'

Rita tiptoed across the deck trying not to get sticky pink paint on her leopard-print boots as she joined Honeysuckle on the prow.

'It's absolutely, completely and positively brilliant!' said Honeysuckle.

Rita hugged her. 'It is, isn't it?' They gazed with delight at their handiwork. The bright glossy colours were dazzling in the sunlight and sparkles from the rippling canal water made The Patchwork Snail look like a glittering fairytale boat.

Honeysuckle turned to her mum. 'Now we could paint something ginormous on the . . .' She paused because Rita was looking at someone on the canal bank. There was a man standing at the edge of their garden, looking at The Patchwork Snail. He wore a grey raincoat – which went almost down to the ground, a brown felt hat and horn-rimmed spectacles held together with sticking plaster. Honeysuckle thought that he could have been a tramp except that he had an official-looking clipboard in his hands and seemed to be making notes.

'Er, can I help you?' Rita asked. The way she asked the question wasn't particularly polite and Honeysuckle could feel her mum stiffen. The man put his hand into his pocket and drew out a business card.

'William Watson from the Waterways Department,' he said, handing it to Rita.

Pink paint smudged from her fingers on to the corner of the card as she took it. She glared at the card and then at William Watson. 'And what can I do for you?' she asked.

'I'm reassessing the mooring rates on this part of the canal and it's come to our attention that the amount of rent you pay hasn't been reviewed for several years,' William Watson explained.

'So?' Rita snarled. Honeysuckle was beginning to feel quite uncomfortable; Rita sounded so unpleasant.

'So, it's probably time that it was reviewed. I need to take some measurements,' the man went on. 'If you have no objection, I'll do that straight away.'

'Be my guest,' said Rita, not sounding at all welcoming.

She folded her arms and tapped her foot while the man from the Waterways stretched his measuring tape across first one bit of the boat and then another. He paced up and down their little garden and quite rudely looked in through the windows of the magic wardrobe.

'Mmm,' he said finally. 'In my estimation, the rent for this mooring should be approximately double what you are paying now.'

Honeysuckle held her breath. She knew that this news would definitely not make Rita happy. She could feel her mum begin to shake and she had a terrible feeling that, at any moment, she was going to explode like a volcano. There was a pause – Honeysuckle noticed that Rita was grasping her right wrist with her left hand and breathing hard.

'I see.' The words squeezed out of Rita's throat as if she was being strangled but she didn't lose her temper. 'And when do you think this rent increase will come into effect?' Honeysuckle saw the knuckles on her mum's left hand going white; she must have been gripping her wrist dreadfully hard.

'I wouldn't be surprised if the increase is backdated – meaning that you now owe the Waterways extra money from several months past.'

'I know what backdated means,' Rita hissed.

'I'll put it all in a letter explaining everything to you,' said William Watson, raising his brown felt hat. 'Good day!' And with that he turned on his muddy heel and marched off towards the town.

Honeysuckle watched William Watson make his way down the path and waited for an explosion. But Rita didn't explode. Instead she slumped down on the prow of the boat and moaned a low, sad moan.

'It'll be all right, Mum,' said Honeysuckle, squatting down and putting her arms around Rita's neck. 'We'll manage, you know we will.'

Rita sniffed.

'We've got loads of dog walking this half-term and I'll be able to give you pots of money – honestly, Mum, please don't worry!'

'Oh, Honeybunch, what would I do without you?' Rita gave a small smile before standing up straight and brushing down her crimson shorts. She tossed her bright orange halo of hair, squared her shoulders and cleared her throat. 'Anyway, we're not going to let some man in a grey raincoat ruin our day, are we?'

'No we are NOT,' said Honeysuckle, jumping up to stand next to her mum.

'No way, José.' Rita grinned. 'In fact, we're going to say "Pink stripes" to the lot of them! And you and I, Honeybunch, will stand united on the deck of our trusty warship and shout, "Get back you dogs" if anyone from the blinking Waterways Department so much as looks at us! What do you say?'

'Absolutely,' said Honeysuckle, grinning back at her mum. 'We'll be like pirates, swishing our swords and shooting our blunderbusses with parrots on our shoulders and treasure in the hold.'

'And in the meantime,' said Rita, 'shall we have a cup of tea and a piece of that ginger cake to celebrate?'

'Aye aye, Captain!' said Honeysuckle, saluting.

'Although I'm not quite sure what we're celebrating,' Rita added.

'We're celebrating our brilliant, newly decorated, wiggly deck!' said Honeysuckle. She made her way very carefully across the deck and down through the hatch into her own brightly painted cabin. Through her cabin was the tiny galley kitchen where Honeysuckle filled the green enamel kettle with water and put it on the stove to boil. She took two rose-printed cups from the row of hooks above the sink and put the teapot carefully down next to them.

While the water heated up, she gazed out of the window across the glittering canal to the bank on the other side. There were clumps of primroses and even from this distance she could make out the pale haze of violets. An emerald-backed mallard duck was busily foraging for food, turning up-tail in the water. His wife spread her wings gently over the chicks in their canal-bank nest. Everything looked so hopeful, so promising. Why did this news have to come today? Why did bad news ever have to come? Honeysuckle knew that her mum already found it really hard to make ends meet. She couldn't imagine what else they could do to save or make money.

Honeysuckle thought miserably that this news almost certainly meant that there would be no exciting trips to the charity shops.

Perhaps I'll get an idea from the tea-leaves, Honeysuckle thought to herself. Maybe there will be a sign. She poured the boiling water carefully over the tea-leaves in the flowery pot, left it to brew for a couple of minutes and then filled the two cups.

She took the cups and the cake back up through the hatch, catching a glimpse of her mum before Rita realised she was there. Just for a moment Rita looked tired – very, very tired. Her hair was all over the place, her eye make-up was still smudged from all the laughter earlier (or maybe she had shed a tear or two while Honeysuckle had been inside) and there was a blob of pink paint on her cheek. The moment she caught sight of Honeysuckle she grinned. 'This boat is a blooming work of art, Honeybunch! Not a pirate ship but a floating palace of prettiness – how clever are we?' They chinked cups. 'A toast!' said Rita. 'A toast to the princesses of The Patchwork Snail!'

As they drank their tea Rita seemed to feel better. Honeysuckle began suggesting plans for the decoration of the prow of the boat. 'And couldn't we use that bit of tiger-print stuff in the shed to cover the deck cushions with?' she asked happily. 'They would look so exotic with these wiggly stripes!'

Rita grinned. 'Abso-blooming-lutely!' she said, hugging Honeysuckle. Nothing appeared to get Rita down for long. But deep inside Honeysuckle knew how worried her mum was about the rent.

When the tea had been drunk, Honeysuckle took the cups back into the galley. She swirled the remains round in her cup and turned it upside down in the saucer. Looking round to make sure that Rita was nowhere near, she peered at the pattern that the tea-leaves had left at the bottom of the cup. 'Phew!' she whistled. It wasn't often that the tea-leaves gave her such a definite picture but this time there was no mistaking it – the shape in the tea-leaves was absolutely, completely and positively a star! 'Now all I've got to do is to work out what it means,' she whispered to herself.

Chapter Three

That afternoon, a few minutes before Honeysuckle
left The Patchwork Snail to meet up with the other Dog
Walkers, she changed her clothes. She wanted to feel as
bright and cheerful as she possibly could. First she
pulled on red velvet trousers with spotty patches on the
knees, then her favourite purple rollneck jumper. After
that she stepped into her flowery Doc Marten boots.
She pinned on her official Dog Walkers' badge and then
gathered some of her hair into two sparkly hair clips.
She looked this way and that at her reflection in the mirror above her tiny dressing table. 'Mmmm,' she said to
herself before plonking a shocking pink beret on the side
of her head. Still not quite content, she fastened several
strings of brightly coloured charity shop beads around
her neck.

'There!' she said to her reflection. 'Ready for anything!' Despite her worries about the man from the Waterways she managed to give herself a brave smile.

'I should be back at about five,' she called to Rita as she reached the deck.

'OK, Honeybunch,' Rita called back. 'Have a good time! Hope those dogs behave themselves!' Rita was perched at the other end of The Patchwork Snail, painting a huge flame-coloured bird on to the stern of the boat. She had tied a purple scarf round her head and her tongue stuck out a little from between her teeth while she concentrated. Honeysuckle watched her mum for a moment. It made her feel horrible to think that she was worrying all the time about money for the rent. She wished there was something she could do.

'Oh, they'll behave themselves all right!' Honeysuckle called back, jumping off the side and on to the grass. As she passed, she noticed that some of her mum's bulbs were just about to burst into flower and her multi-coloured primulas were gleaming through the shadows. Even though the little gnome in the corner of the garden was a bit shabby, the rest of the garden looked lovely.

Honeysuckle ran up the steps and crossed the road. She walked up the path to Mrs Whitely-Grub's red front door; it looked so welcoming and friendly.

'Ah, there you are my dear,' Mrs Whitely-Grub greeted Honeysuckle. 'Little Cupie is all ready for his walkies – aren't you, my beautiful boy?'

Cupid was bouncing up and down with his blue bow bobbing around on the top of his head. He knew that if Honeysuckle was here he was going to go out on an adventure and he was extremely excited.

Honeysuckle looked down at Cupid. 'Steady boy,' she said, ruffling his topknot. She felt Mrs Whitely-Grub's eyes on her and looked up.

'Is everything all right, my dear?' asked Mrs Whitely-Grub, meeting Honeysuckle's gaze.

'Um . . . yes, um, I suppose . . .' Honeysuckle replied. Then, for no reason that she could properly explain, she began to cry. Great big fat hot tears welled up in her eyes and slithered down her cheeks.

'My dear, why don't you come in, just for a second?'

And that was when Honeysuckle told her the whole story about William Watson, the man from the Waterways, and the things he had said about their rent. The elderly lady couldn't have been sweeter, and although she didn't suggest anything that would help, it made Honeysuckle feel better just to have told her everything.

By now Cupid was desperate to begin his walk and Honeysuckle explained that she had to go to Jaime's house to meet the others before collecting the rest of the dogs.

'You must be on your way then, my dear. And try not to worry,' said Mrs Whitely-Grub.

Honeysuckle smiled bravely although she didn't see how she was supposed to stop worrying. She and Cupid set off into the town.

Just walking along the streets with the little poodle on his lead and her official badge pinned on her front made Honeysuckle feel better. She loved the sound his claws made as they tap tapped on the pavement, and the feeling that he depended on her to look after him. She could stop whenever she felt like it and pat him or give him a cuddle. And if he was especially good, she could reward him with a biscuit. Honeysuckle knew that she would never be able to have a pet of her own on The Patchwork Snail. Rita said that even a teeny weeny hamster or a goldfish in a bowl would take up too much space.

When she reached Jaime's ramshackle house the others were waiting outside for her. 'Yo, Abba fan!' called Billy and Honeysuckle grinned back at her three good friends.

Jaime was wearing her old dungarees and, as usual, her hair was in a complete tangle. She had a striped scarf that was probably Billy's wrapped round her neck and a lollipop in her mouth. 'Ooo all wight?' she tried to ask with the lollipop still in her mouth. She pulled it out and tried again. 'You all right?'

Honeysuckle nodded. Jaime looked hard at her but didn't ask anything more.

'So, who have we got today?' Anita asked anxiously. She always worried that they would have more dogs than they could cope with. Honeysuckle explained that there were four dogs, one for each of them, so everything would be fine.

'Is Pudding coming?' Anita asked.

'Yup,' said Honeysuckle. 'You can take Pudding if you like.' She knew that Pudding was Anita's favourite because he had very short legs and a big tummy and couldn't walk very fast. This meant that Anita was usually at the back of the group, where she felt safest. It seemed weird to Honeysuckle that her friend wasn't nervous of swimming for her county in championship races but that she was nervous about almost everything else.

'You have brought some poo bags, haven't you?' Anita

asked with her forehead all puckered.

'Don't worry,' Honeysuckle said. 'I always have poo bags in my pocket – since Cupid did you-know-what on the pavement that very first time we took him out.'

'Phew!' sighed Anita.

As they set off towards Pudding's home, Billy kicked a tin can down the street while providing a running commentary. 'And he's coming up to the goal posts now . . . he's dribbling the ball, carefully does it . . . he aims . . . he shoots . . .' – here Billy kicked the tin in between two gateposts that they happened to be passing – 'AND IT'S A GOAL!' he shrieked, leaping up and down and waving his arms in the air.

Honeysuckle sighed. Boys could be very exhausting. Not that Billy was nearly as bad as lots of the boys that she knew. And besides, he was Jaime's best friend – not her boyfriend, absolutely not – but her best mate.

Jaime giggled as Billy shot his goal and then she turned to Honeysuckle. 'Are you sure you're OK?' she asked. 'It's just that you look a bit, you know, as if you might have been crying or something.'

Billy and Anita both turned to look properly at Honeysuckle. 'Yeah,' said Billy, 'I noticed that.'

Honeysuckle had to smile – he obviously hadn't

noticed anything of the sort, but she knew he was trying to be kind. 'I'll tell you in a minute, when we've collected all the dogs,' said Honeysuckle, as they were just coming up to Pudding's home.

Once they were on their way, Pudding waddled next to Anita and Blossom the bloodhound padded along with Billy. Jaime and the little Yorkshire terrier, Hamlet, who was last to be collected, wiggled down the road together.

'Now tell me,' demanded Jaime, grinning, 'or I'll set the dogs on you!'

Honeysuckle tried to make a joke of the funny tramp of a man from the Waterways. 'I'm William Watson,' she said, mimicking his voice and the way he had stood with his feet sticking out at right angles. 'And I think your rent should be raised and backdated.' She knew she didn't need to explain how hard it was going to be for her mum to find the money to pay more. She told them that she and Rita were going to defend The Patchwork Snail to the bitter end.

'We'll all help!' said Billy. 'He sounds a real loser. D'you want me to go and beat up this Waterways geezer for you?' He said this while punching the air like a boxer. 'I easily could – or I could set his feet in concrete and throw him into the canal!'

'Shut up, Billy,' said Anita. 'That's really horrible.'

'Can't you suggest anything helpful?' Jaime asked him.

Billy looked blank.

'I don't think there is anything anyone can do,' said Honeysuckle unhappily. 'Unless we blindfold him and make him walk the plank . . .'

'Yeah!' said Billy.

'I was *joking*,' Honeysuckle told him. 'I suppose we might have to stop living on The Patchwork Snail and rent a room or something cheaper somewhere else.' She looked miserable – she was remembering the time she thought her mum had wanted to move into a house with her boyfriend, Sergeant Monmouth. The others looked glum too: they loved The Patchwork Snail; all Honeysuckle's friends thought it was the most exciting place to live.

'How awful,' said Anita. 'You could come and stay at my mum and dad's house,' she added, brightening. Honeysuckle gave Anita's arm a squeeze but she didn't reply.

The four Dog Walkers walked gloomily along for a while, not saying much, each wrapped up in their own thoughts. Then Billy suddenly stopped, grinned and blurted out, 'I know this isn't going to help, but it might distract us a bit. I think there's something interesting happening on the common – I saw trailers and caravans as I went past last night. Why don't we go and have a look? The dogs would like it and it might take your mind off things for a while.'

'Wicked!' said Honeysuckle, looking up with a smile. The Dog Walkers and their four dogs turned left and began to walk towards the common.

Chapter Four

They took the path through the broad patch of woodland that surrounded the common so that the dogs could have a run, although in Pudding's case it was really more of a waddle. Billy was out in front with Blossom the bloodhound; he threw a stick for her to fetch but Hamlet the Yorkie kept beating her to it.

Honeysuckle tried to keep her mind on the dogs and not think about the depressing Waterways man. The woods looked beautiful, with new leaves unfurling and primroses spangling the mossy banks. And it was warm in the honey-coloured sunshine. She didn't want that beastly Waterways man to spoil such a perfect day.

She was in charge of Cupid who needed to be kept on his lead. He looked all sweet and innocent but the Dog Walkers knew from bitter experience that he would be down the nearest rabbit hole in the twinkling of an eye if they gave him the chance.

'Do you think they've had enough yet?' panted Billy. For the past ten minutes he and Jaime had been playing fetch with Hamlet who, despite being very small, was easily the most energetic of the four dogs. Hamlet still looked full of beans but Billy was puffed out.

'Shall we just run them all round to the other side of the common?' Honeysuckle suggested. 'And then we'll be able to see if the trailers you saw are still there.'

'OK,' the others agreed, and they set off. Running the dogs round wasn't as easy as it sounded. Blossom, who was huge (and truthfully Honeysuckle's favourite) didn't really 'do' running. She did more of a slow trot, while Pudding plodded slightly faster than usual. Hamlet hurtled and Cupid pranced on the end of his lead, like a ballet dancer.

'Look! They're still there!' Billy shouted. 'In fact, I think there are even more trailers and caravans and stuff today than before!'

The others came panting up behind him.

'What's going on, d'you think?' wheezed Jaime, having finally caught up with Hamlet. 'It isn't the fair, is it? There aren't any rides or dodgems or anything.'

'Let's go over and have a closer look,' suggested Honeysuckle.

'Do you think we should?' asked Anita. 'We won't be trespassing or anything, will we?'

'You can't trespass on the common,' said Jaime. 'That's why it's called the "common" – it's common ground for everyone.'

'Oh, OK then,' Anita agreed, and she and Jaime and Billy clipped the dogs back on to their leads.

As they got closer to the first group of trailers, Honeysuckle noticed a huddle of people standing out in the middle of the cricket pitch. 'What are they doing?' she whispered.

'You don't think there's been a murder, do you, and these are all the police and detectives who've come to investigate?' Anita squeaked.

'Yeah – look, there's a mangled body under that tree!' Billy teased. 'Don't be daft,' he said. 'If there had been a murder, there would be all that blue and white tape round everything and we wouldn't be able to get anywhere near.'

'Well, why are all those people standing in a huddle like that then?' Anita asked.

'I think they're discussing something,' said Jaime.

'Oh,' she went on excitedly, 'look over there!'

The others looked in the direction she was pointing. 'What?' said Honeysuckle. 'What is it?'

'That man over there,' squealed Jaime. 'He's that actor, isn't he . . . Isn't he the detective in that series on TV, you know – thingamebobble? D'oh! What's it called?'

'I can't see him,' said Billy. 'Let's get a bit closer.'

The Dog Walkers took a few steps nearer the action. 'You're right,' Billy spluttered. 'It's *Inspector Codey*!'

Honeysuckle suddenly remembered the star in the bottom of her teacup – it must have meant that she was going to see a *TV* star! She smiled a little to herself. She *did* have fortune-telling powers!

The four Dog Walkers stood spellbound as they heard a voice shouting, 'All right people! Back in your places please . . .' and from the middle of the huddle on the cricket pitch a woman appeared. She was joined by a man wearing a suit and a soft hat.

The huddle scattered across the grass, taking make-up boxes and hairbrushes with them. The woman smoothed down her cream-coloured dress and clasped her hands in front of her. She stood herself before the man in the suit.

'Cameras roll!' called another voice.

'This is truly dreadful,' the woman began. 'The Inspector must never be allowed to see . . .'

The Dog Walkers didn't get to hear what the Inspector must never see because at that moment Cupid decided to bark. Loudly.

'Oh my God! Quick, let's hide behind here!' squealed Anita, and she pulled the others behind the nearest trailer. 'We'll be killed for messing up the scene.'

Honeysuckle poked her head out from behind the trailer. The woman was shouting. 'How can I *possibly* be expected to work under conditions like these? There should be *total silence* while I make my speech! How *dare* you let anyone sneeze, let alone BARK, while I'm delivering my lines . . .' And with that she began to stalk off across the cricket pitch.

'But *darling*,' cried a man who Honeysuckle was pretty certain must be the director, 'it's all part of the plot! You knew there were going to be dogs – there may well be barking – it's perfectly all right!'

'It might be all right for *you* but I am not prepared to work with *amateurs* . . .' she shouted, and she flounced off and climbed noisily into a big trailer on the edge of the cricket pitch, slamming the door hard behind her.

'Whoa,' gasped Anita. 'That was scary! But why did Cupid bark like that?'

'I think it was the sight of *him*,' whispered Honeysuckle, pointing to a dark figure that had just stepped out from behind the next-door trailer.

At the sight of the figure Cupid, on cue, barked again. The man looked fleetingly at them and then walked off in the opposite direction. 'He looks creepy,' said Jaime. 'I wonder who he is?'

'Well,' said Honeysuckle, 'whoever he is, Cupid doesn't seem to like him.'

'And dogs have a sixth sense about people, don't they – like Ms Moribunda's dog, Twitter, when we went on that ghost hunt – they know when things aren't right,' whispered Anita.

'Mmm,' murmured Honeysuckle.

'Whatever,' Jaime said. 'I don't care who he is; it's amazing to have this TV crew and actors and everything here – on our common – don't you think?'

'I wonder how long they'll be here for?' Anita asked. 'Shall we come again tomorrow and see what's going on? I can't believe that I've really seen *Inspector Codey* in real life! And that lady with the gloves – I'm sure I've seen her in something else as well.'

'Yeah,' agreed Billy, 'it's awesome!'

Honeysuckle didn't say anything. She was scratching Blossom's ear.

'What are you thinking about?' Jaime asked her.

'Oh,' said Honeysuckle. 'I was just wondering . . . Do you think the actors are very well paid?' she asked quietly.

'Probably,' Jaime answered and then she frowned. 'You're really worrying about the Waterways man, aren't you?'

Honeysuckle nodded. 'I'm sorry, I can't stop thinking about it. My mum works so hard already. I don't see what else she could do to make more money.'

'Perhaps we could help?' suggested Anita.

'Yeah,' said Billy. 'We could give her all our dog walking money!'

'That's brilliant, Billy!' Jaime and Anita agreed.

Honeysuckle felt a lump in her throat. She blinked back her tears and said, 'That's so sweet of you guys but the point is that the dog walking money is for you; you've earned it. And anyway, I think we would have to walk a zillion dogs to make anywhere near enough.'

'There must be *something* we could do to help,' Jaime said.

'We could rob a bank,' Billy suggested. 'You guys could

lower me on a rope through the skylight of the bank in the High Street and I could work out the combination on the safe and nick the dosh!'

Honeysuckle giggled. What was it about boys, she wondered, that made them think there was nothing in the world that they couldn't do?

'Meanwhile, we'll be hanging on to the end of the rope and trying not to slip off the roof, I suppose?' teased Jaime.

'You'd have to wear those special boots,' Billy said, 'with suction pads on the bottom. And after I'd got enough money out of the safe – because we wouldn't need it all – you could winch me back up on to the roof and no one would ever suspect —'

'You're such a goof,' Anita said.

'I was just trying to help.' Billy shuffled a pebble with his toe.

'I can't see you as a bank robber somehow!' Jaime said, giving him a pretend punch. 'There must be something we could do that isn't illegal.'

'In the meantime, let's get off the common,' suggested Honeysuckle. 'We don't want the dogs disturbing the filming again.'

'If we can keep the dogs quiet, maybe if we go back

again tomorrow the director might see us and ask one of us, or maybe ALL of us to be on the show – what do you think?' said Anita excitedly, as they walked back towards town.

Honeysuckle looked at her with her eyes wide. 'Oh!' she gasped. Perhaps that was what the star in her tea-leaves had meant! Perhaps it was she, Honeysuckle Lovelace, who was going to be the star! Maybe that was the way she was going to make enough money to pay the rent for their mooring!

When all the dogs except Cupid had been delivered safely back to their owners, Honeysuckle said goodbye to the others. They had all agreed to go back to the common the following day in the hopes of getting themselves discovered.

As Honeysuckle walked back through the tree-lined streets to Mrs Whitely-Grub's house she felt a little glow of excitement – she was already making plans for the following day.

Chapter Five

When Honeysuckle woke up the next morning the sun was creeping in between her spotty curtains. She sat up with a start. What time was it? she wondered as she grabbed her alarm clock. Eight o'clock! She shook her mane of black curls out of her eyes and tried to remember what it was that she had to get up for. She had been dreaming that she was walking up a red carpet wearing the most beautiful dress imaginable. There were hundreds and thousands of people each side of the carpet all cheering at her and blowing kisses. There were flashbulbs popping left, right and centre as Honeysuckle posed for the cameras, smiling and laughing and feeling fantastically famous.

'Of course,' she said, bouncing out of bed. 'The TV crew!' She pulled on her bright blue dressing gown and called out, 'Hello? Mum, are you here?' There was a groan from the cabin at the other end of the boat.

'What's the matter?' asked Honeysuckle, making her way through into the galley kitchen. It was perfectly possible to have a conversation with her mum wherever she was. That was one of the good things about living on a houseboat – it was so small that you never had to shout to be heard. It was friendly and cosy even though there wasn't enough room for lots of the things that other people took for granted.

'Oh, Honeybunch!' Rita screeched. 'I can't find anything to wear that doesn't clash with my hair!' She popped her head out through her cabin door. 'Look at it. I should never have agreed to let Nev dye it this, this *fluorescent* orange! What am I going to do?'

Honeysuckle thought it was weird that her mum was suddenly worried about the colour of her hair – it had never worried her before.

'I can't dye it a different colour because he'll threaten to walk out again . . . Aarrgh! Men! Why are they all so blooming annoying?'

Now Honeysuckle thought she understood. It wasn't really Nev from the Curl Up and Dye salon that her mum was angry with, it was much more likely to be the man from the Waterways. She knew her mum was trying to pretend that she wasn't worrying about the rent.

'I think you look gorgeous,' she said as Rita came through into the saloon of The Patchwork Snail. She was wearing skinny blue jeans with diamanté sprinkled down the seams, a bright pink jersey and a red and pink swirly patterned scarf tied round her head in a big bow. She had put on her dangly 'diamond' earrings (bought for twenty-five pence in Oxfam) and on her feet she wore lipstick-red ballet shoes.

'Thank you, Honeybunch!' Rita said, flinging herself down on to the velvet-covered bench seat in the saloon and beginning to practise her deep breathing. In between breaths she asked, 'What are you up to today?'

'Well . . .' Honeysuckle began. 'We've got four dogs to walk this afternoon . . .'

'You're brilliant, Honeybunch, you really are,' Rita said. 'You'll be a millionaire yet! I just wish you could think of something that your old mum could do to bring in the money.'

Honeysuckle looked sadly at her mum before telling her about the TV crew on the common.

'Oh yes,' Rita said. 'Cindy in the salon was talking

about that the other day – she said she'd heard they were going to make an episode of *Inspector Codey* here, in town. So it's all happening, is it?'

'Yup,' said Honeysuckle. 'It's really exciting – we saw Steve Milligan yesterday, you know, the man who plays the Inspector?'

'Oh yes,' said Rita. 'He's the one Cindy thinks is DEEEEE-VINE! I better not tell her that he's around or she'll never be able to concentrate on the shampooing!'

'We thought we might go and see if we can get, you know, Discovered, by the director!' Honeysuckle explained. 'So I'm going round to Anita's in a minute to work some things out. Sorry I won't be able to help with the rest of the painting.'

'That's OK, Honeybunch,' said Rita, who suddenly didn't seem to be listening. 'You go off. I need to buy some paintbrush cleaner anyway before I can start and I ought to just check in on the salon.' She got up and walked through the galley towards the steps that went up from the far end of Honeysuckle's cabin to the hatch and on to the deck. Honeysuckle thought her mum looked distracted, as if she wasn't really concentrating on what she was doing. 'Be sure to leave everything shipshape,' she called as she climbed up the steps. Then she added, 'Oh for goodness' sake! I haven't got my purse,' and she scuttled back into her cabin.

By the time Rita did actually leave, Honeysuckle had drunk her first cup of tea. She swirled the remains around, tipped the cup upside down and looked at the remaining tea-leaves. 'Hmm, that is a very interesting shape,' she said to herself as she turned the cup this way and that. Honeysuckle wanted the shape to look like a star again or perhaps even an acting trophy. But no matter which way she looked at it, the only shape she could possibly see was a light-bulb! What on earth would a light-bulb mean? She sighed and rinsed her cup under the tap. Perhaps the shape didn't mean anything; perhaps on this occasion it was just a blob of tea-leaves after all.

She bustled about getting herself ready for the day ahead. She washed and dressed in her most film-star-like outfit, which consisted of a green skirt with silver bobbles round the hem, black tights, a white fluffy jersey with extra fluff round the neck, her sparkly red butterfly hair clips and her usual flowery Doc Marten boots.

She turned this way and that in front of her mirror, practising her TV-star smile. 'No, I'm sorry,' she said to an imaginary fan, 'I never give autographs – but you may kneel and kiss my hand if you like . . .'

She practised flouncing like the actress on the set had done the day before. She thought that her flounce was much more impressive. She delivered her Oscar acceptance speech – it was so moving she almost made herself cry.

When she had finished flouncing and giving interviews, she piled a huge selection of hair bobbles, ribbons, necklaces, hats and badges into her backpack. 'Right,' she said, addressing the green-backed duck as he floated past her window. 'THIS is my big chance to make loads of money!'

Honeysuckle turned and bounded up the stairs, through the hatch and on to the deck. She slammed the hatch shut and leapt on to the bank humming 'Super Trouper' happily to herself. When she reached the pavement she glanced back at The Patchwork Snail. It really did look fabulous with its bright, shiny paint. Before too long, Honeysuckle felt certain that she would be able to pay as much rent as William Watson from the Waterways could possibly want.

By the time she reached the modern bungalow where Anita lived she was completely out of breath. She had rushed through the town, eager to tell the others all about her plans.

'Phew!' she gasped, falling in through Anita's door. 'Hiya! I've had loads of ideas for things we could do to get Discovered. Are the others here?'

'They're in the sitting room,' said Anita, giving Honeysuckle a hug. 'Come on, tell us what you've thought of.' She led the way into the large, bright room that had windows all down one side and a wall full of shelves all down the other. Anita's swimming trophies were lined up on the shelves: Honeysuckle could hardly believe how many she had won.

She turned to look at her friends. 'Wow!' she said. 'You guys look fantastic!'

Jaime had actually brushed her hair and she was wearing a *skirt*. Honeysuckle didn't think she had ever seen Jaime in a skirt before – even at school she always wore trousers. She was amazed, and a little bit envious, of her friend's long slim legs.

Then she turned her attention to Billy. He was wearing exactly what he had worn the day before – scruffy ripped jeans, a T-shirt and a very beaten-up leather jacket; the only difference was that he had slicked back his hair and was chewing gum noisily.

Anita looked her usual clean and shiny self except that, for once, she had untied her long auburn hair. It rippled down her back like a sheet of copper. 'I brought these in case anyone wanted to borrow anything,' Honeysuckle said, emptying her backpack on to the floor.

While Anita and Jaime decked themselves with Honeysuckle's baubles and beads, they all began to discuss what they could do to get themselves noticed by the director of the film.

Before Honeysuckle had a chance to suggest any of her ideas, Billy said, 'I could do my Elvis thing.' He swivelled his hips and sang, '*Are you lonesome tonight . . .*'

'Shut up, Billy! Be serious!' Jaime grinned.

'You could be my backing singers,' said Billy, ignoring her. '*Do you miss me tonight . . .*'

'OK, OK, Billy,' said Honeysuckle, grinning too. 'What about using the dogs?' she asked the others.

Billy was well into the second verse now so Jaime had to shout her reply. 'Perhaps we could use the dogs in some sort of rescue scene – you know, something dramatic that would impress the director.' She giggled, pinning a big pink flower into her hair.

Billy was suddenly quiet while he strummed on his air guitar.

'Well,' he said, abandoning his Elvis pose. 'We've got Blossom this afternoon and she looks like the sort of dog that could swallow a person whole, doesn't she? Perhaps we could make out that she was about to attack Anita, and the rest of us could rescue her from the jaws of death!'

Jaime laughed. 'And then you could sing a bit of Elvis, I suppose, once Anita is safely rescued!'

Honeysuckle giggled. 'And we *could* be your backing singers . . . although it might be a bit odd if Anita is meant to be slightly horribly mauled . . .' They were all laughing now, except for Anita.

'Blossom won't really be attacking me, will she?' she asked anxiously.

'Anita!' the other three cried in unison. 'You know what Blossom's like – she wouldn't hurt a fly. It's just *pretend*, you know, *acting*,' explained Jaime.

'Oh, I see!' said Anita, looking confused. 'Do you think we should practise a bit, without the dogs, before we go?'

Honeysuckle knew that her friends were trying their best to stop her thinking about her problems. She grinned and said, 'Brilliant plan! Positions please, *actaws*!' and pointed to where she wanted her friends to stand for the practice run. 'Now, after three, Anita lie on the ground groaning – try to look as if you are about to be eaten . . . Billy pretend to be mega strong and drag Blossom off her and Jaime, you look horrified, like this,' – here Honeysuckle did her best horrified look – 'See? And then scream a bit . . . OK? After three – one, two . . .'

'What about you? What will you be doing?' asked Jaime.

'Oh,' said Honeysuckle, making a dramatic terrified gesture. 'Don't you worry, I'll be screaming too!'

Chapter Six

'You know that bit we thought we would do in front of the director, where Anita is being eaten by Blossom?' asked Jaime as they walked Blossom, Hamlet, Twitter and Splodge towards the common that afternoon.

'Well, not *eaten* exactly,' said Honeysuckle, giggling, 'but yes, you mean the bit where Anita is moaning and groaning in agony and you and I are screaming. What about it?'

'What if someone really thinks that Blossom is attacking Anita? They might take her away and lock her up or even, even . . .' Jaime swallowed hard.

Honeysuckle gasped. 'Oh no! I hadn't thought of that! That would be dreadful!'

'Why don't we make Blossom rescue Anita instead?' asked Billy. 'Anita could get lost or fall over or whatever and Blossom could find her and then we could all sing something together?'

'Yeah,' said Jaime. 'That sounds better! And maybe while we sing we could do a dance routine and the dogs could perform tricks and things . . . except that they don't know any.'

Anita, who still didn't seem to have got the joke, interrupted. 'Why is it always me who has to fall over or get lost? Why can't I be a brave and fearless hero for once?'

''Cos you're *really good* at being a victim,' said Billy seriously, which for some reason made Anita look much happier.

They were passing the Curl Up and Dye hairdressing salon and Jaime suddenly said, 'Oh look! There's your mum!'

Honeysuckle peered in. Her mum wasn't supposed to be in the salon now. She was just going to drop in for a moment that morning on her way to buying paintbrush cleaner before going back to The Patchwork Snail.

'Oh,' said Anita as the four Dog Walkers stopped outside the salon's huge window. Through the window Honeysuckle could see her mum quite clearly. She had her hands over her face and Nev had his arm round her shoulders.

They were all quiet for a moment. Honeysuckle felt wretched. Her mum was trying so hard to be bright and cheerful when they were together. But here she was actually *crying* when she thought Honeysuckle couldn't see her. Jaime gave Honeysuckle a hug. 'Come on, there's nothing you can do here – let's go and try and get Discovered by the TV director and then we can come and tell your mum that you're going to be a superstar and all her troubles are over!'

Honeysuckle did her best to smile. 'You're right,' she said. She gave herself a little shake. 'Shall we get a bit nearer to the common and then put some of my ribbons round the dogs' necks and give them a brush and stuff?'

'Yeah,' said Jaime. 'Bags I do Twitter.' Jaime and Twitter the whippet had become really good friends since the ghost hunt and even though his owner, Ms Moribunda, had moved to a different house, she still asked the Dog Walkers to take Twitter out. Jaime stroked his pale, fine coat and fastened a red bow round his neck. 'There!' she said proudly.

Although Honeysuckle would have liked to groom Blossom, she let Billy do it. He thought being with the smaller dogs made him look like a 'right wuss', but

Blossom, he had decided, was more of a 'man's dog'.

Anita was in charge of Splodge, who was a very old and rather smelly bulldog. He had a lovely squidged up face and a little curly tail, like a pig's. She chose a yellow ribbon for him and tied it in a huge bow behind his left ear.

'We all look so beautiful!' exclaimed Honeysuckle when she had finished smartening Hamlet up. She tried to put all her worries to the back of her mind. 'Come on,' she said, with a dramatic sweep of her arm and putting on her 'actaw's' voice. 'Let's go to the common and get Discovered!'

There were even more trailers and caravans parked around the cricket pitch when the Dog Walkers arrived. There were scruffy vans that had all the technical stuff in them, like cameras and sound recording equipment. Men in black T-shirts were scurrying backwards and forwards between the vans, with rolls of wire and microphones. Then there were trailers with *Wardrobe* printed on the side where all the costumes must have been kept. There was a mobile canteen and some really posh silver trailers where Billy said he thought the actors hung out.

They noticed a group of people on the far corner of the pitch but as far as any of the Dog Walkers could see there was nothing being filmed at that moment.

'Why don't we do something dramatic now?' asked Jaime. 'We can use the middle of the cricket pitch so everyone will be sure to see us.'

'Do you think the director is over there?' asked Anita, pointing to the group.

'I bet he is,' said Honeysuckle. 'He's probably telling the cast right now how desperately he needs brilliant, fresh, young talent and a group of dogs to put in the TV series – let's go!'

'Shall we just walk across first,' said Jaime, 'and try to attract everyone's attention?'

'Right on,' replied Billy, and he set off across the cricket pitch doing the slow, slouchy walk that he thought made him look cool. Blossom padded beside him followed by Honeysuckle and Hamlet. Jaime and Anita came along behind with the other dogs. No one from the group surrounding the director took the slightest notice.

'Fat lot of good this is doing,' growled Billy.

Anita, who still didn't really understand that the bit about her being a victim was a joke, decided it was time to do her piece of acting. Very slowly and dramatically, she dropped to her knees and then rolled herself gently over on to the grass. Splodge was rather taken aback by this and let out a howl. He seemed very concerned and stuck his squished up face with its wet, pushed-in nose and slobbery, wobbly jowls right into Anita's. Anita was so surprised that she screamed. The others burst out laughing, which only made Splodge howl even louder. This in turn made Blossom bark, which set Twitter and Hamlet off as well. The noise was deafening.

'Well if this doesn't get us noticed nothing will!' said Jaime, gasping for breath.

All four Dog Walkers stopped laughing and turned, hopefully, towards the group surrounding the director.

'Not one single measly person is looking our way,' said Honeysuckle. She stood and stared across the grass with her hands on her hips. 'What do you think we have to do to get noticed around here?'

'Beats me,' said Billy, slicking back his hair and taking up an Elvis-style pose.

'Oh this is useless,' puffed Jaime.

'I thought I was doing really well, but it's all been for nothing!' Anita wailed.

The dogs, having been mystified by the strange

behaviour of their walkers, had stopped barking and were all sitting quietly on the grass next to Anita. Jaime plopped down next to them and Honeysuckle joined her. Only Billy stayed standing. He was playing air guitar in a last ditch attempt to get the film crew to notice him.

'It's useless, Billy,' said Honeysuckle. 'Come and sit down – we'll have to think of something else.'

'They must all be idiots,' Billy said as he joined the girls on the grass. 'Can't they recognise potential talent when it's looking them straight in the face?'

'Exactly,' Honeysuckle said. She rested back on her elbows and looked up into the watercolour-blue sky. The plump, cushiony clouds drifted slowly by while she tried to think of another plan.

She was just about to suggest that they got up and did a routine from *Grease* in a final attempt to get noticed when Jaime said, 'Oh my God! You know who that woman is, don't you?' The others looked to where she was pointing. The actress they had watched the day before was walking towards the director. 'That's Suzie Storm! I didn't recognise her yesterday with her costume on! I can't *believe* that I'm this close to Suzie Storm! She is just so cool!'

'It is!' squeaked Anita. 'Do you think she's seen us?

Oh, I loved her in *Secrets and Spies* – she was amazing!'

'Blimey,' said Billy. 'The guys in the football club will be knocked senseless when they know I've seen her – she isn't cool, she's *hot*!'

Honeysuckle thought that she hadn't been so hot the day before, when she was having a tantrum. But suddenly she saw something that made her squeak. 'Almost as hot as Guy Mount!' Honeysuckle pointed excitedly. 'Look! There he is over by the catering caravan! Ooooh! He is *gorgeous*!'

'Oh,' said Anita, 'I think I'm going to faint! I feel all wobbly and peculiar – I *love* Guy Mount . . .'

'Shall we go over and say "hello"?' Jaime suggested.

'I think I might just wander over in that direction and introduce myself,' said Billy, pointing towards Suzie Storm and the director.

'You can't do that!' Anita squealed. 'We might get thrown off the common, or anything!'

'Do any of you dare go and say hi?' Jaime asked. The others were silent. Even Billy seemed to have lost his nerve.

'We could let one of the dogs run over there and then go and sort of rescue it as if it was a big accident and then when we get close up we could say, "Oh! I didn't realise it was YOU! Could I have your autograph?" or something like that,' Honeysuckle suggested.

'I don't think we better do that,' Anita said. 'Look, they're just about to begin rehearsing another scene.' She was right: Suzie Storm and Steve Milligan were looking at their scripts and the director was asking for quiet.

'There must be some way that we could get to meet them,' Honeysuckle whispered, as they began to lead the dogs off the common.

She had been so excited about seeing famous actors that for a few moments she forgot about The Patchwork Snail and her mum. But as they walked back into town, Honeysuckle started dragging her feet; her heart felt so heavy, weighed down by worries. She still hadn't found a way to help Rita get more rent money.

She had been wrapped up in her own thoughts, not listening to the others as they walked along, but suddenly Billy's voice made her jump. 'Hey! Have you seen this?' He was standing with Blossom by the newsagent's window.

Honeysuckle and the others joined him. 'What? What is it?' Jaime asked.

'This!' Billy shouted. 'This notice!'

The girls crowded round.

'*Wanted,*' Honeysuckle read, '*for the filming of an episode of* Inspector Codey. *Extras are urgently needed. If you can spare the time please come to the common on Wednesday 5th at 9.30 a.m. for filming that day. Dogs with their owners will be particularly welcome.*

'That's tomorrow!' Honeysuckle spluttered. 'They want extras with dogs tomorrow! That's us! We can do that!'

'We really will be on the telly!' said Jaime breathlessly.

'And meet Suzie Storm,' Billy added, trying to sound cool about it but not convincing any of the girls.

'*And* Guy Mount!' said Anita dreamily.

'Not only that – they'll pay us loads of money too!' Honeysuckle exclaimed.

It was all so exciting that the Dog Walkers had to have a group hug, which confused the dogs and started them barking.

'We're going to be stars after all!' said Honeysuckle above the din. She posed dramatically with one hand on her hip and the other ruffling her hair. Everyone laughed.

The Dog Walkers gave each other high fives before agreeing where to meet the following day. As Honeysuckle and Hamlet turned back towards the canal she felt her heart lift. She still didn't understand the sign that she had seen in the tea-leaves that morning but now she was pretty certain it must have something to do with being on TV.

Chapter Seven

'Ten, nine, eight, seven . . .'

'Mum, what are you doing?' asked Honeysuckle. Rita was sitting on one of her tiger-print cushions on the newly painted deck of The Patchwork Snail with her eyes closed, counting backwards. It was still early in the morning but the sun was already glowing. Rita had positioned herself in a warm spot between the purple shadows.

'Shh!' she hissed. 'Six, five . . .'

'You woke me up,' said Honeysuckle. 'I didn't know what was going on.'

Rita opened her eyes and scowled at Honeysuckle. 'I'm trying to go to my Special Place and that needs concentration, so if you don't mind . . .'

'Why do you need to go to your Special Place?' asked

Honeysuckle, who was still too sleepy to realise she was being annoying.

'BECAUSE,' sighed Rita, 'I was going to have the day off but now I can't and I woke up wanting to smoke just one little ciggie, just one, mind, or even to have one tiny puff . . .' – she mimed blowing smoke into the air – 'and I'm trying to make the feeling go away before I succumb to the filthy filter tips again.'

'Was that what made you want to smoke – not having the day off?' asked Honeysuckle, yawning. She rubbed her eyes and looked properly at her mum. Rita looked pale and worried and Honeysuckle noticed dark smudges under her eyes.

'Oh, you know, that and other things . . .' Rita's voice trailed off.

'You mean the man from the Waterways and the rent thing?' Honeysuckle asked, sitting down next to her mum and giving her a hug.

'Well,' Rita replied, 'I suppose it might have had something to do with William Watson esquire . . . But don't you worry, Honeybunch, I'm sure I'll think of something. Anyway,' she went on, 'I'm so excited to think that you are going to be in *Inspector Codey*! Imagine, my own girly being on the telly!'

'I bet they'll pay us loads!' said Honeysuckle. 'And maybe they'll want us in every other episode as well!'

'You're not to worry about money, Honeybunch,' Rita said seriously. 'It's down to me to look after you, not the other way round.'

'OK,' said Honeysuckle. 'But I thought I might do a little bit of "Dancing Queen" to get the director to notice me!' She jumped up and began an Abba-style dance routine. Rita laughed and joined in and The Patchwork Snail rocked to and fro.

'You're going to be on the telly!' Rita sang as she wiggled. 'I'm SO proud of you! Well done!'

Rita was still grinning when she suddenly looked at her watch and said, 'Ooops-a-blooming-daisy! I should be on my way to work!' She swooped back down the hatch and reappeared moments later with her sparkly chandelier ear-rings glittering in her ears and her huge orange bag over her shoulder. The bag matched her hair exactly and Honeysuckle thought her mum looked amazing.

Rita kissed Honeysuckle goodbye and told her to leave everything shipshape.

'Aye aye, Captain.' Honeysuckle saluted as her mum jumped off the boat and disappeared in the direction of town.

Honeysuckle hummed a little to herself as she got ready for the day. She whizzed round the saloon, plumping up the flowery cushions on the velvet-covered bench seat, straightening the strings of beads that were hanging across the windows, washing up her breakfast things in the tiny galley kitchen and finally standing in front of the mirror in the world's smallest bathroom, brushing her teeth. As she brushed, her eyes wandered round the exotic pictures that she and her mum had painted over the slightly mouldy walls. There was the mermaid with her curling tail and the weird and wonderful fish that looked like brightly coloured sweeties swimming through the azure waves. Honeysuckle loved every centimetre of The Patchwork Snail.

She went back into her tiny cabin and pulled on her cut-off blue jeans over her sparkly silver tights. She wanted to be sure that the cameras wouldn't miss her so she chose the brightest red top she could find. Then she popped her feet into Rita's red ballet shoes. They were a bit big and probably not the most practical thing to walk dogs in, but Honeysuckle wanted to get her look right. She pinned four pink and red flowers into her hair and finished the outfit off with seven coloured bangles, three sparkly brooches and her Dog Walkers' badge.

Honeysuckle gathered up the things she needed for the day before climbing the stairs to the hatch and letting herself out on to the deck. It was one of those sparkling spring mornings when it's hard to believe that anything horrible could ever happen.

The other Dog Walkers were ready and waiting for Honeysuckle at the top of the stone steps that led from the canal to the road. They grinned at each other.

'Don't we look awesome?' said Jaime, gazing at each of them in turn – and it was true. They had all dressed themselves in their starriest clothes and even Billy had put on a clean T-shirt and a pair of mirrored sunglasses. Jaime had given up on her skirt idea and was wearing her favourite jeans instead but with a sparkly T-shirt. Anita wore a plain blue skirt and a buttercup yellow zip top.

'OK guys,' Billy said, 'this is it – our chance to hit the big time.' He straightened his sunglasses and ran his hands through his hair. 'No messing around today, this is serious!'

'Yeah,' Jaime agreed. 'We have to do this really well and make sure that we get noticed.'

'For being the fabulous superstars-in-the-making that we really are!' Anita interrupted.

'Exactly,' Jaime continued. 'So Billy, no more Elvis?'

'No more Elvis.' Billy nodded. 'Today I'm gonna be my normal cool self . . .' The girls giggled. 'I'm gonna work hard,' Billy went on, 'and make shedloads of money! Enough money to keep a whole fleet of house-boats afloat!' he said, turning to Honeysuckle.

'Billy, you can't give what you earn to Mum and me!' Honeysuckle gasped.

'Course I can,' said Billy. 'Famous superstars – or even not-so-famous extras – can do whatever they like with their money and I'm going to help save The Patchwork Snail.'

'Me too,' Jaime and Anita added.

Honeysuckle had to pinch herself. She mustn't cry. She couldn't turn up on the film set with a bright pink nose and smudgy eyes. 'You guys are so sweet . . .' she said, clearing her throat and sniffing a bit. 'So how much do you think they'll pay us?'

'It's sure to be lots, isn't it?' Anita asked. 'I mean film stars are always fantastically rich, aren't they?' The others agreed excitedly. As they set off arm in arm to collect the dogs, they were all certain they were about to make the biggest pile of money any of them had ever seen.

There were five dogs to be walked that day: Cupid, Pudding, Hamlet, Blossom and Splodge. Honeysuckle said that she would take Cupid and Hamlet and leave the others with one dog each. That way, she felt certain, they would be able to perform really well in front of the director.

As they got closer to the common they were amazed to see loads and loads of people all swarming in the same direction.

'What are all these people doing, do you think?' Anita asked.

'They're not all coming to be extras, are they?' Jaime said incredulously.

Honeysuckle's heart sank a little. She really hadn't expected there to be quite so many people. 'Never mind,' she said as cheerfully as she could. 'It'll be us that the director picks out – we've got the dogs!'

Honeysuckle thought fleetingly about the light-bulb she was sure she had seen in the tea-leaves the day before. She still couldn't work out what it might mean. Perhaps it was something to do with the filming today and she was about to find out . . .

'Would all you people here to be extras line up on this

side of the cricket pitch?' a voice boomed through a megaphone.

'That's us!' said Honeysuckle. 'Let's go!'

They found themselves in a huge crowd of people, some with dogs but most without, being herded across the grass away from the other actors and the place where the director sat.

They had to line up in front of the trailer with *Wardrobe* printed on the side. Here two women checked their clothes. Honeysuckle felt a pang of disappointment when she was given a dull overcoat and realised that her cut-off jeans and bright red jersey wouldn't be seen. And they told her to take the the red and pink flowers out of her hair.

'It's just so you don't stand out in the crowd,' one of the women explained when she saw Honeysuckle's expression.

When the whole crowd of extras was ready, a man with a megaphone shouted at them for what seemed like hours. They were told to move first one way and then the other and then to stand and chat to each other.

They didn't see a glimpse of a single star and Billy never got to be quite as cool as he had hoped. In fact, as soon as the cameras started filming, he got terrible stage fright and couldn't move at all. Honeysuckle realised what was happening to him and wished that she could suggest some of the things her mum did to help her stop smoking – like counting backwards and going to a special place in his head. But she couldn't tell Billy to do that now. 'Don't be scared,' she whispered when she thought the camera wasn't on them.

'I'm not scared,' said Billy with his teeth chattering. 'I just can't move, that's all! Anyway, this is dumb – no one is going to discover me dressed like this, I'm giving up.' He pulled off his coat. 'They'll just have to pay me for half the time, that's all! I'll take Blossom off for a wander round the common and see you later,' he said, secretly hoping that he might bump into Suzie Storm along the way and that she might beg him to be her leading man.

Honeysuckle had to agree that being an extra was not quite what she thought it would be. All they had to do was walk across the common and stop from time to time to pretend to chat to each other. By the time they got to the eighth take, she decided that being a star was not nearly as exciting as she had first imagined. For one thing, the director never even looked at them. For another, they were nowhere near the stars they were so longing to meet. And for another thing, she was desperate to go to the loo.

'Take nine!' the man with the megaphone shouted and off they went again. This time Honeysuckle had to walk with her legs crossed and she was so fed up that she stuck her tongue out too, just for good measure. Strangely, the megaphone man seemed happy and eventually shouted, 'Cut! Thank you people! It's a wrap!'

Honeysuckle flung Cupid and Hamlet's leads at Jaime and said, 'Back in a minute,' before rushing to the nearest Portaloo.

When she came out, Anita and Jaime were waiting. 'I feel such a numpty,' she said. 'I stuck my tongue out on that last take and that's the one they're going to use!'

'It doesn't really matter though, does it?' said Jaime unhappily. 'I mean, it's not as if anyone could really see us amongst all these people anyway.'

'No, that's true. Still,' she said, trying hard to be positive, 'I expect they'll pay us in a minute.'

But Honeysuckle was wrong. It turned out that they were paid nothing for being extras. They were just supposed to do it 'for the fun of it' as the man with the megaphone grumpily explained when they asked.

Now Honeysuckle really did have to try hard not to cry. She couldn't believe it! It had never occurred to her that they wouldn't be paid.

Jaime gave Honeysuckle a hug and a little tickle to cheer her up. Anita put her arm through her friend's as they made their way across the common.

'What a blooming swizz,' said Jaime. 'We never even caught the tiniest glimpse of Guy Mount or Suzie Storm or anyone else for that matter!'

'I wonder what Billy's been up to?' said Honeysuckle, blinking back her tears. 'Maybe *he's* been schmoozing with Suzie Storm while we were being a crowd.'

But she was wrong about that too. Billy caught them up and told them what he'd been doing. He had wandered off with Blossom and had found himself right on the edge of the common where there was only one trailer, all on its own. He had recognised the creepy man that Cupid had barked at two days before, coming out of the trailer. It turned out that his name was Dirk and that he was a dog trainer. It was his job to train three dogs to 'act' in the thriller. Billy said he wasn't *that* creepy once you got talking to him and that he had shown Billy how he got his dogs to do tricks.

'Oh well,' said Honeysuckle sadly. 'At least *you* got something out of the morning!' The others looked at her. They had all hoped so much that they would make some money and be able to help Rita pay the mooring rent – but they hadn't made a single penny.

'Don't worry,' Anita said, squeezing Honeysuckle's arm. 'I'm sure we'll think of something . . . soon.'

Chapter Eight

With the dogs safely delivered back to their owners, the Dog Walkers made their way to Jaime's house. They sat in her untidy kitchen and munched their way through fat, doorstep sandwiches while they thought about what to do next. There was no one else in the house so they had the whole, lovely ramshackle place to themselves.

'Come on,' said Jaime in between mouthfuls. 'There must be something we can think of to make shedloads of money.'

'Hmm,' Honeysuckle said. She had been gazing through the open kitchen door at a clump of daffodils outside. There was dew on their petals and the drops glittered like diamonds.

'Honeysuckle?' Anita prodded her and Honeysuckle

jumped. 'You were miles away.'

'Oh, sorry,' said Honeysuckle. 'I was just thinking . . .' She decided not to tell her friends that she was thinking how much she loved The Patchwork Snail and how she absolutely, completely and positively didn't want to move. 'I was just thinking that I wish Mum could win the lottery or something.'

'Well that's about as likely as me being able to do maths,' said Jaime who was utterly and totally hopeless at maths. Honeysuckle smiled.

'I could do a sponsored swim!' Anita suddenly said. 'I could go round and ask people to sponsor me to swim, oh I don't know, ten miles or something!'

'Ten miles?' Billy gawped. 'How are you going to swim ten miles?'

'Ten miles isn't that far . . .' Anita said. 'People swim from England to France all the time and that's much further . . . I could work out how many lengths of the public pool it would take and then . . . and then . . . SWIM it!'

'But who would sponsor you?' Jaime asked. 'I mean, mostly people sponsor things that are for charity . . .'

'And my mum would absolutely, completely and positively *hate* being thought of as a charity case,' said

Honeysuckle. 'But it was a lovely idea,' she added quickly as Anita looked a little upset, 'and I know you could do it, easily.'

They carried on munching in silence until Jaime said, 'Couldn't we collect money just to save The Patchwork Snail? I mean that doesn't sound like a charity, does it?'

'Well . . .' began Honeysuckle.

'Because I could do all sorts of things to raise money,' said Jaime excitedly.

'Like what?' Billy asked.

'Like . . . like . . . sitting in a bath full of baked beans!' said Jaime triumphantly.

'Eew!' Anita said, but Jaime was off with her mad idea growing more and more possible in her head. 'I could get the baked bean company to pay me! It would be really good advertising for them!'

'How?' asked Billy, who was looking fed up because he hadn't come up with an idea of his own.

'It would prove that baked beans are not only yum to eat but good for your skin as well!' Jaime announced.

'Are they?' Anita was frowning anxiously. 'That's not really the point of them, though, is it?'

'No, but it's an added bonus,' Jaime explained.

Honeysuckle thought how lucky she was to have such

good friends, even if they were a bit bonkers. 'That's a really good idea,' she said kindly.

'GOT IT!' Billy shouted. He jumped up from the table. 'I'll go busking with my band!'

'What band?' Anita asked. 'I didn't know you had a band!'

'Yeah!' Billy said. 'There're four of us – I do bass guitar and the lead vocals.'

'Oh!' the three girls said together. They all knew Billy could sort of sing the low parts when they sang things all together but none of them thought that singing was what Billy was best at. He started crooning quietly and Honeysuckle thought that she'd better change the subject before it all got embarrassing. But there was no stopping him; he was twanging wildly on his air guitar and giving a full-blown rock star impersonation – at least, Honeysuckle thought that was what it was meant to be. Both she and Anita tried to ignore him but Jaime couldn't help jiving round the kitchen table and drumming a bit on the bread bin.

'Ooooh!' she said, grinning. 'This could really be it, Honeysuckle, don't you think?' She stopped a moment to make a spectacular drum roll while Billy gyrated madly. 'It could be AMAZING!'

'Well . . .' Honeysuckle said uncertainly. Anita had joined in with the others now and was throwing her arms in the air, doing some kind of weird old-fashioned jive. That was too much for Honeysuckle – she had to join in too. She grabbed Anita's hand and whizzed her round until they were facing each other. Then they swung easily into one of their favourite dance routines. They bopped and hopped and jumped and shook while Jaime crashed away on the bread bin and Billy yelled his favourite boy band hits at the top of his voice.

'Wowzers!' Jaime whistled, after about half an hour of full-on drumming. Honeysuckle and Anita flopped down on two of the many huge cushions that were piled in a corner of the kitchen.

'I thank you, fans,' Billy said, bowing to an imaginary audience. He raised his hands as if he was trying to quieten a clamouring crowd and then in his best American drawl he said, 'I thank you. I know you'll want to give everything you've got to this lil' lady over here . . .' – he gestured towards Honeysuckle – 'to stop her lil' ol' home from going under . . .'

'The Patchwork Snail isn't sinking!' Honeysuckle said, giggling. 'At least I don't think it is!' She was puffed out but, although she was laughing, she didn't really feel any happier. 'The thing is, I think you are all brilliant, and I love all your wicked ideas for making money, but . . .' She hesitated. What she was going to say might sound ungrateful and she didn't want it to. 'But I have to think of something that will help us for ever and ever, not just for the next few weeks.'

'I know, but we will think of something, I know we will . . .' said Anita.

As she made her way back towards the canal, Honeysuckle felt exhausted. All the fun of being Discovered and meeting the stars had gone wrong and she still had William Watson from the Waterways to worry about. She stared around her at the softly swaying trees: some were bright with fresh new leaves; others were heavy with blossom and petals fluttered down like confetti as she walked beneath them. Lots of the houses she passed had window boxes full of harlequin-coloured primulas and there were tulips making vibrant clumps of colour in people's front gardens. The air was sweet with the scent of spring flowers and everyone Honeysuckle passed smiled contentedly.

By the time she arrived back at the canal, it was already quite late. Rita, back from work, was on the deck of the houseboat surrounded by pots of paint. 'Hiya, Honeybunch!' she called. 'Look, it's all finished!'

Honeysuckle grinned. The Patchwork Snail was bobbing about on the canal smothered in gorgeous rainbow-coloured flowers, butterflies and the occasional gold star, which Rita had splashed on just for good measure.

Honeysuckle bounced on to the deck. 'It's fabuloso!' she said. 'I love the starry bits!'

'Well, that's what we are, isn't it? Little stars! Especially you! How did the filming go?'

'Oh,' Honeysuckle said, feeling as if a bubble had suddenly burst. 'It was all hopeless. We didn't get to meet any of the actors and the director didn't even notice us!'

'Honeybunch! What bad luck,' Rita said. 'So you didn't even get a proper look at Guy Mount or that lovely Steve Milligan? Cindy will be disappointed!'

'Mum!' Honeysuckle squeaked. 'Steve Milligan is OLD! We wanted to see Guy and Suzie Storm but, like I said, we didn't see anyone AND . . .' She hesitated a moment as Rita stared at her. 'And,' she went on sadly, 'we weren't paid any money!' Honeysuckle thought she saw her mum's shoulders slump a little just then. 'We did make quite a lot dog walking though,' she added quickly.

'Honeybunch,' Rita said, shaking her head so that her earrings twinkled in the late evening sun. 'I've told you: you are not to worry about money; it'll all be fine.'

They had home-made pizzas with salad for supper as a treat to cheer themselves up. The evening was just warm enough to eat out on the deck of The Patchwork Snail and watch the spring sun dip slowly behind the distant hills. As it disappeared, the sky turned from pale blue to crimson and then back to darkest blue. Honeysuckle listened to the water lap gently against the sides of the boat and felt the soothing sway of the canal.

By the time she had washed and got herself ready for bed, she had made up her mind she was going to look in her crystal ball and see if she could find any of the answers she needed. As the crystal ball had to be kept a secret from Rita, Honeysuckle quietly closed the door of her cabin before she began.

The crystal ball was about the only thing her dad had left her. She had found it when she was six. It was under a pile of bits and pieces at the back of the magic wardrobe in a cardboard box with her name on it. Even at that age she understood that this was a secret, something between her and her absent father, something that her mum must never know about.

She took the magical globe from its secret hiding place in the drawer under her bunk bed and unwrapped the beaded midnight-blue velvet from around it. Placing the ball carefully on to its wooden stand she polished the gleaming surface with the sleeve of her pyjamas and peered into the crystal depths. Nothing. She waved her hands over the ball, the way she had seen people do in films, and looked again. Still nothing, except . . . except that the darkness in the centre of the ball seemed to be growing darker as Honeysuckle looked. It was like a black fog swirling in the crystal's sparkling centre. Honeysuckle blinked and just for a moment she thought she saw something like a piece of paper with a list written on it. The image was gone in an instant but suddenly, as if by magic, a Brilliant Idea popped into her head.

Chapter Nine

It was amazing that Honeysuckle managed to sleep at all that night, with her head so full of her Brilliant Idea. Once it had popped into her brain she couldn't imagine why she hadn't thought of it before.

In between tossing about on her lacy pillow and dreaming brightly coloured, extraordinary dreams, Honeysuckle realised what the light-bulb shape in her tea-leaves had meant. 'Of course!' she whispered into her moonlit cabin. 'A light-bulb means having an idea! Just like in cartoons! How dumb am I? The tea-leaves were predicting that I was going to have a Brilliant Idea!'

By the following morning, Honeysuckle had made some important decisions. The first was not to tell her mum anything about her Brilliant Idea, just in case it all went wrong. The second was to go and see Mrs

Whitely-Grub as soon as Rita went to work and the coast was clear. The third decision was to tell Jaime and Billy and Anita all about her plans and to ask them if they would help her.

'You're up bright and early, Honeybunch!' Rita said as Honeysuckle scrambled out of the world's smallest bathroom, wrapped in her pink bath towel. 'Didn't you sleep well?'

'Not very well,' Honeysuckle answered honestly.

'Oh life is so unfair,' Rita wailed, looking hard at Honeysuckle. 'If I have a bad night, I look like a three-hundred-year-old bag lady for at least the whole day – but if you have a bad night, you look as bright and fresh as a dew-splashed daisy. How can that be right?'

Honeysuckle giggled.

Rita went on. 'In fact, you look brighter and smilier than I've seen you look for days. What's going on?'

'Oh, nothing much,' Honeysuckle replied as casually as she could.

'Nothing much?' Rita repeated. She moved closer to Honeysuckle and tickled her under her chin. 'Are you telling your old mum the truth? You're not IN LOVE are you?'

'Mum!' Honeysuckle squeaked. 'Of course I'm not in

love! I'm just . . . just happy, that's all! It's a beautiful morning and we've got Cupid and Splodge to look after today and it's going to be fun – that's the truth!'

'Hmm.' Rita smiled. 'Well, I'm really pleased to hear that you're feeling happy, but I can read you like a copy of *Hello!* magazine and the headlines are telling me that *Something is Going On*! Although, since you are obviously not going to tell me, I shall just have to imagine that you have made a wicked plan to kidnap Guy Mount and keep him all to yourself in the magic wardrobe!'

'Yup!' Honeysuckle laughed. 'That's exactly right! How did you guess?'

Rita chuckled as she put the finishing touches to her make-up before leaving for the salon. Honeysuckle noticed her mum's smile fade. She didn't look like a three-hundred-year-old bag lady but she did look tired. Rita smacked her cherry-coloured lips together and said, 'I might be a bit late tonight, I've got a couple of extra heads of highlights to do – I need to pack in as many as possible. When will you be home?'

'Oh, I'll be back before you then,' Honeysuckle replied. 'We take the dogs back at four.'

'That's great,' Rita said, searching under the rose-print

cushions for her other earring. 'Now which shoes . . . ?'

Honeysuckle thought her mum would never leave. She was all dressed and had eaten her breakfast by the time Rita was actually ready for work. She finally rushed up the steps shouting, 'Leave everything shipshape, won't you, Honeybunch?'

And at last Honeysuckle was able to shout, 'Aye aye, Captain,' and know that she could get on with her important plans.

She needed a notebook so she pulled the green Dog Registration book out from one of the drawers under her bunk bed. There were lots of pages at the back that she could use. She found a pen and made her way out of The Patchwork Snail and across the road to Mrs Whitely-Grub's house.

Once they had quietened Cupid down, Honeysuckle was able to ask the elderly woman's advice. Mrs Whitely-Grub was quite ancient but, because she was so old, she knew about a lot of interesting things. When Honeysuckle told her about her Brilliant Idea, Mrs Whitely-Grub knew exactly how to go about making the idea work. They sat together in the old lady's sitting room and drafted out a very carefully worded letter. When they were both satisfied that the letter said precisely what it needed to say in the most businesslike way, a whole hour had passed.

They took the drafted letter to the library where they were able to type it out properly on a computer. Once they had the printed letter in front of them, Mrs Whitely-Grub patted Honeysuckle's hand and said, 'I think it's a wonderful plan, my dear! I'm sure you will get plenty of support and I will do everything I can to help. In fact, this is the first thing I can do . . .' She signed her name in spidery black writing at the bottom of Honeysuckle's letter. 'There!' she said. 'Now off you go and see how you get on – you'll let me know, won't you, how it's all going?'

Honeysuckle grinned and gave the old lady a kiss on her cheek. 'Thank you!' she said. 'Shall I come back to your house and take Cupid with me now? I'd be happy to have him for the whole day, if you like?'

Mrs Whitely-Grub agreed that on this particular day it would be a great help to know that Cupid was being looked after, as she wanted to do some shopping in town and meet an old friend for lunch.

Honeysuckle skipped with Cupid down Mrs Whitely-Grub's path and then they made their way towards Anita's house.

When she arrived, Jaime was already there with Anita. They told Honeysuckle that Billy was at football practice.

'Never mind,' Honeysuckle said. 'We could go down to the pitch and meet him there. Now, Anita, have you got a clipboard?'

'Yes, but what do you want a clipboard for?'

As Honeysuckle was about to burst with the excitement of her Brilliant Idea, it was wonderful to be able to spill the whole thing out to her best friends. She told them about the tea-leaves and how she hadn't understood the signs; then she told them about the picture that looked like a list in her crystal ball. 'And that's when I realised that I should do A PETITION!'

'What do you mean?' Jaime asked, scratching the back of her tangled hair with a pencil. 'I don't understand – what will a petition do?'

Honeysuckle took the Dog Registration book out of her bag, in which she was keeping the printed letter safe, and showed the letter to Anita and Jaime. 'You see, I'm going to ask people to sign this letter stating that the mooring rates for The Patchwork Snail shouldn't increase. And then,' she went on, 'when we've got loads of signatures we can take the petition to the mayor and hope that public demand will make him do something about it. So we won't need to make shedloads of money, because, hopefully, the rent won't go up.'

'When we've got loads of signatures?' Jaime asked, frowning.

'Oh, er, I knew there was something I forgot to say.' Honeysuckle blushed. 'Do you think you might help me?' She looked from one friend to the other. 'You see, I think it's my only hope.'

She felt her heart thumping before Anita and Jaime both said together, 'OF COURSE we'll help!'

'And Billy will want to help too,' Jaime said, 'I'm certain. Let's go and find him now!'

The girls took the letter and tore several sheets of paper out of the book, 'Just in case . . .' as Anita put it, and clipped them on to the clipboard. They tied a pen to the board with a piece of string and set off, with Cupid, towards the football pitch.

On the way, Honeysuckle explained that she hadn't told her mum anything about her Brilliant Idea; she wanted to be absolutely, completely and positively certain that it would work before she did that. 'It will be just horrible if this plan goes wrong – especially as I can't think of any other ways of making money. No, stopping the rent going up has to be the answer!' She tried to sound confident; if her petition didn't work, then the future of The Patchwork Snail looked very, very gloomy indeed.

Billy was bright red and covered in mud when they found him. He was puffing and panting on the edge of the pitch as the training session had just finished. He thought the petition idea was totally cool. Straight away he said, 'Give me the clipboard for a mo . . .' and dashed off towards the other players and their coach. When he came back to the girls he had eighteen signatures.

'That is amazing,' Honeysuckle said, grinning until her cheeks hurt.

'Not really,' Billy said gruffly. 'Everyone round here knows The Patchwork Snail, they all think it's wicked – kind of part of the scenery, a national landmark – and they want to help.'

Honeysuckle might have given Billy a huge kiss right then and there if he hadn't been quite so hot and sweaty. As it was, she said, 'Thank you, thank you . . .' about fourteen times until Billy held up his hand and in his best American drawl said, 'That's OK, fans . . . the least a handsome superstar can do!'

'Yeah, yeah, whatever,' Jaime said, trying to bring him back down to earth. 'Why don't you go and wash and then we can start getting some more signatures?'

'Right on,' Billy said, before bounding off across the pitch to the changing rooms. By the time he came out, scrubbed and shining, the girls had realised that they could ask all their dog walking clients to sign the petition as well. As they had to go and collect Splodge, they got his owner, Mrs Poole, to sign first before making their way round the town and visiting all the other dog owners. On the way, they passed a few people in the street who were happy to sign too.

Having given Splodge a good waddle before taking him back to Mrs Poole, they returned to the canal with fifty-eight names in all. 'Not bad!' said Billy, although for the past hour they had only managed to get two new signatures.

Honeysuckle was beginning to have doubts. Maybe fifty-eight was all the names they would get. Would that be enough to convince the mayor to lower the mooring rent? She had hoped that they would get at least a hundred people to sign . . .

Noticing Honeysuckle's anxious face Jaime said brightly, 'We'll have to start the next sheet of paper now! *And* we haven't even tried our other school friends or the people who work at the salon yet!'

Honeysuckle did her best to smile but there was still a quiver of fear in her stomach.

When they had delivered Cupid safely back to Mrs Whitely-Grub, Jaime and Anita thought they deserved a treat. They could see that Honeysuckle needed cheering up so the two girls sent Billy off to buy ice cream while they put the tiger-print cushions out on the deck of The Patchwork Snail. Honeysuckle was careful to hide the clipboard so that Rita wouldn't spot it when she got back from the salon. She would have to think of a way to get Nev and the others to sign the petition when her mum wasn't at work.

While they lazed on the tiny deck of the houseboat, slurping ice cream and making plans for the following day, Honeysuckle suddenly noticed a familiar-looking man wandering along the footpath. 'Isn't that . . . ?' she gasped. The others turned to see where she was looking. 'It is! It's the director of *Inspector Codey*!' Before she had time to think what she was doing Honeysuckle jumped up and waved. The director smiled back, and, although he obviously didn't know who Honeysuckle was, he wandered slowly towards the boat.

Honeysuckle sat down with a bump and put her hand over her mouth. 'Why did I do that?' she mumbled. But it was too late to worry about it as the director was right up beside the boat now and it looked certain that he would say something to her.

'This is very beautiful!' He pointed at The Patchwork Snail. 'Did you do all this painting?' he asked, looking at each of the Dog Walkers in turn.

'No,' Billy answered when it was clear that no one else was going to say anything. 'She did it with her mum.' He pointed at Honeysuckle. 'It's their houseboat.'

'It's fantastic,' the director said, smiling broadly.

'Thank you,' said Honeysuckle, suddenly finding her tongue. 'But you see, the thing is, that the man from the Waterways wants to put the mooring rent up and we won't be able to afford to stay here . . .' – once Honeysuckle had started she didn't seem to be able to stop – 'so, my friends and I have started a petition . . .' – Jaime scuttled down through the hatch to grab the clipboard – 'and we're trying to collect as many names as possible to say that the rent shouldn't be made more expensive . . .' Jaime reappeared with the petition and handed it to Honeysuckle. 'Do you think you might sign it for us?' she asked, pushing the clipboard towards the director.

As she held it out towards him, Honeysuckle saw

that her hand was shaking, but the director didn't seem to notice. He took the board and said, 'Of course I'll sign your petition. I tell you what, I'm making a film on the cricket pitch . . .' The Dog Walkers nodded politely, as if they didn't already know this. He took a tiny camera out of his pocket. 'I'll take a picture of your wonderful boat and show the cast and crew on the set. If you come round tomorrow, I'm sure they would all be happy to sign too. Just come to the director's trailer and ask for Greg – that's me!'

Chapter Ten

Not telling Rita about the petition and the director's visit to The Patchwork Snail was one of the hardest things Honeysuckle had ever had to do. From that point of view, it was lucky Rita was so exhausted when she got home from work. All she had done was to eat a little supper before flopping into her bed. At least there hadn't been too much time to discuss what Honeysuckle had been up to during the day.

Although she opened her eyes while the spring sun was still rising in the sky, by the time Honeysuckle was properly awake Rita was calling, 'Leave everything shipshape, Honeybunch!' All Honeysuckle saw of her mum that morning were her bright pink high-heeled stilettos disappearing out through the hatch of the boat.

Honeysuckle rubbed her eyes and tumbled out of her

bunk. She skittered around like an excited puppy. She put on the kettle, had a bath and washed her hair, made tea and got dressed in record time. But it was still much too early for the others to arrive. Honeysuckle doubted that the cast and crew of the TV film would even be awake at this hour of the day.

'Now what are you going to do?' she asked herself severely. 'You are such a numpty to get up so quickly – there's still ages to go until nine o'clock.'

Honeysuckle put on an Abba track and sang along. *'Dancing queen, you are the dancing queen, ooooh, ooooh . . .'* It didn't matter how hard she tried to concentrate on the song, all she could think about was going to the common and meeting the TV stars. She couldn't even work out what the tea-leaves in her cup looked like. They seemed to be making the shape of a necklace, but that made no sense at all, so Honeysuckle swished the cup out and left it to drain.

She danced back into her cabin. *'Dig it the dancing queen . . .'* she sang into the mirror above her tiny dressing table. When she was completely satisfied that she looked businesslike but as sparkly and colourful as possible, she set about tidying her cabin.

Getting things in the right places always helped to

make Honeysuckle feel calm. She arranged her hair bobbles and put her bangles into her pale blue leather jewellery box. She straightened the fairy lights hanging over her bunk and pulled the lacy cover up over her carefully tucked-in bedclothes. Then she plumped up the sequined cushion that sat at the head of the bed and folded all her clothes and shoved them in the flowery orange cupboard above it.

After what seemed like a lifetime to Honeysuckle, the boat began to rock. A head poked through the hatch. 'Hiya!' Jaime said, and a moment later Billy's head appeared as well. 'Anita's waiting by the gnome,' Jaime explained. 'Shall we go?'

Honeysuckle was so excited about taking the petition to the common that she had almost forgotten the four dogs they were walking that morning. By the time they had collected Splodge, Twitter, Blossom and Hamlet, it was all she could do to stop herself running flat out to the cricket pitch. Billy slowed them all down. He was determined to be cool about the whole thing and slouched along with one hand in his pocket, whistling. It didn't take a psychologist to work out that he was only pretending not to care. Anyone could see that he had gelled his hair and put on a clean T-shirt, which for Billy was quite something.

When they finally got to the common, they made their way straight to the director's trailer. The others told Honeysuckle to knock on the door; they said it was her petition so she should be the spokesperson. Her knees shook a little as she climbed the steps.

Before she even reached the door, it flew open. 'Good morning!' Greg, the director, beamed at the Dog Walkers. 'Great to see you all! And all these dogs! Where did they come from?' When Honeysuckle had explained about the Dog Walkers' Club, Greg said, 'You should go and see our dog trainer – he's as good as a magician with dogs, can make them do *anything*!' Honeysuckle was going to say that Billy had already met the dog trainer when Greg asked if they had the petition with them. Honeysuckle nodded and showed him the clipboard.

He smiled and said, 'I'll get everyone out to meet you! I showed the photo of your houseboat around last night and I think you'll get a good response . . .'

By now Greg was down the steps and marching across the grass to the centre of the cricket pitch. He had a megaphone in his hand and the Dog Walkers and their dogs scuttled along behind him. Putting the megaphone to his mouth, the director shouted, 'Listen up, people! I have the owner of that glorious houseboat here with her petition – please come and sign your names! Could save a family from losing their home . . .'

Already Honeysuckle could see trailer doors opening and people making their way across the grass towards her. First there were lots of technicians who were really friendly and made jokes while they signed their names. Then Steve Milligan himself came and signed. Honeysuckle wished Rita could have been there to see him. He was so nice – although he was much shorter than he looked on TV.

After him, there were several people who Honeysuckle thought must be actors although she didn't recognise them. She couldn't believe how many people there were! They just kept coming and the number of names on the list grew and grew, over one page and on to the next and then the next . . .

'Oh my God!' Anita squealed and shot behind Billy. She peeped out from over his shoulder and said, 'It's HIM! Look! It's Guy Mount and he's coming over! Ooooooh, I can't stand up!'

'Shut up, Anita,' Billy said, stepping sideways. 'Gotta try and look cool . . .'

He was doing his best to look as if chilling out with the stars was something he did every day when Honeysuckle hissed, 'And there's Suzie Storm!'

Billy gulped. He ran his fingers through his gelled hair and went into such a cool slouch that he almost fell over.

Suzie Storm looked gorgeous and not at all as if she was about to have a tantrum. She went straight up to Billy and asked him where the petition was. Poor Billy was starstruck and stood gaping, unable to make a sound.

Jaime stepped in and pointed to Honeysuckle, who was surrounded by people. 'It's just here. If you would like to sign, that would be awesome!'

Guy Mount had stopped for a moment to talk to the director, but now he was head of the queue to sign Honeysuckle's petition. She gazed at him; her eyes were filled with stars and her smile felt as if it was stretching from one ear to the other.

'Hello!' he said.

'Er . . .' Honeysuckle replied.

'Shall I sign here?' Guy Mount asked.

'Um . . .' Honeysuckle managed to say.

'I've seen your wonderful houseboat, you know,' Guy said. 'I walked past it the other day. It's quite a landmark!'

Honeysuckle blushed. Guy Mount had walked past her home? He knew where she lived? She felt her mouth flop open and somehow she just couldn't close it again.

Guy Mount smiled at her. 'Perhaps you could give me the pen?' he said, carefully prising the pen out of Honeysuckle's clenched fingers.

'Mmm,' Honeysuckle replied.

'It's a beautiful houseboat,' Guy said as he signed his name.

His name! Honeysuckle thought. He's signing his name on *my* petition! But, just like Billy, not one word would come out of her mouth. As he finished crossing the 't' at the end of his name, Guy looked up, still holding the clipboard. There was a sound of popping flashbulbs and Honeysuckle realised that there were press photographers all around them. Guy smiled his most handsome smile and Honeysuckle did her best to pull herself together.

'Mr Mount,' one of the reporters shouted. 'Could you tell us about this petition and why you think it's important to sign?'

He gave the clipboard and pen back to Honeysuckle with a wide grin. Then he sauntered across to the reporters. She heard him begin to tell them about the 'marvellous houseboat, a terrific asset to the area . . .' before she found Suzie Storm standing in front of her tickling Hamlet's ear.

The morning was like a dream, over in the twinkling of an eye. Honeysuckle didn't think she could ever forget how kind and friendly everyone had been and how willing they were to help. All these really important, well-known people understood how horribly frightening the thought of a rent rise was to her and her mum and how much The Patchwork Snail meant to them both.

When the queue of people, the reporters and press photographers had moved away, the Dog Walkers and their dogs were left with Greg. 'You could have a wander round the trailers over that way,' he said, gesturing to the furthest part of the common. 'See if anyone got left out – you're sure to find a few stragglers!'

Honeysuckle hardly knew how to begin to thank him. She and the others did their best before they began to wander, dazed and starstruck, across the common.

They did find a few more people to sign the petition and they also found the dog trainer again. Billy introduced them all to Dirk, who seemed friendly, although there was just something about him that Honeysuckle didn't like. He had four dogs with him, which worried

Blossom who hung back, hiding behind Billy. Splodge and Hamlet were happy enough to meet Dirk's dogs but they steered well clear of Dirk. Twitter shook and trembled and wouldn't go near him.

Dirk showed them a few of the tricks he had trained his dogs to do. He told them that it was important to show a dog who was the boss and then they would do exactly what they were told. 'I can get my dogs to do anything,' he said. 'Anything at all that I ask them . . . they're like my little slaves . . .'

'He might be able to get his dogs to do anything,' Honeysuckle commented while they walked back towards the town, 'but he can't write his name very clearly, can he?' She peered at the squiggle Dirk had made on their list.

'But hey! Look how many signatures we got!' Jaime said.

'All those actors . . .' Anita said dreamily. 'And the photographers! There'll be photos of us and everything!'

'Hope they got one of me and Suzie,' Billy said. No one said it but each of the girls hoped for Billy's sake that the photos wouldn't be in colour – his face had been SO red.

As they passed the Curl Up and Dye salon, Honeysuckle

managed to signal to Nev. She beckoned him outside, making sure that Rita didn't catch sight of her and told him all about the petition. Nev got very excited and emotional and promised to get everyone in the salon to sign if Honeysuckle left it with him. He gazed at the TV stars' signatures and clutched the clipboard to his chest as if it was the most precious thing he had ever held.

'Promise you won't let Mum see it?' Honeysuckle begged. Nev promised and Honeysuckle did her best to believe him.

'You know what we should do now?' Jaime said, as they delivered Splodge, the last dog, back to his owner.

'No,' said Honeysuckle. 'What?'

'We should make banners and placards to take to the Town Hall with the petition.'

'So we can have a demonstration when we give it in?' Honeysuckle gasped, her spirits soaring. 'Of course! That is a Brilliant Idea!' She hugged Jaime. 'Almost as brilliant as mine!'

Chapter Eleven

Billy might have been a bit of a goof about some things but he was very, very good at making placards.

The four friends spent the next couple of hours in Jaime's kitchen doing exactly what Billy told them. He said that he'd helped his cousin make anti-war banners so he knew how they should look.

They ended up with four placards. *DOWN WITH MOORING RENTS* was written on one; *RENT RISES UNFAIR* on another and on the third Honeysuckle had printed *WATERWAY BULLIES*. Billy's banner read *SAVE THE PATCHWORK SNAIL*, which Honeysuckle felt really said it all.

While they worked, they discussed their morning and all the famous people they had met. 'Suzie Storm didn't look as if she would ever have a moody fit, did she?' Anita said. The others agreed that she had been very nice and friendly in real life. Billy didn't say anything but Honeysuckle noticed his cheeks going pink again.

The girls discussed Guy Mount for a while before having an argument about whether his eyes were blue or green. Billy, who had been finishing off his banner, said, 'Who cares about his blinking eyes?'

Honeysuckle laughed before suddenly feeling that flutter of fear in her stomach again, as she looked at the placards. What if none of this worked? What if the demonstration was a useless waste of time? She started to feel sick with anxiety. Her phone beeped, snapping her out of her mood. There was a message from Nev. *Need to talk — where are you?* it said. Honeysuckle texted back explaining where she was and within moments Nev had replied that he was on his way over.

By the time Nev arrived, the Dog Walkers had lined their finished placards and banners up against the kitchen wall and were admiring their handiwork.

'Ooh!' Nev said, bursting in through the back door. 'Those look ever so professional, I must say!' He was breathing heavily as if he had been rushing to get there.

'Listen, ducky,' he said to Honeysuckle. 'I managed to get everyone to sign the petition without your mum noticing that anything was going on.'

'That is so brilliant, Nev, thank you!' Honeysuckle said, taking the clipboard from his hand.

'I must say,' Nev continued, 'I think you did a *marvellous* job getting all those TV personalities to sign! Cindy wanted to give me her diamond engagement ring in exchange for Steve Milligan's autograph! Wouldn't her Bobby be pleased, I don't think!'

Honeysuckle giggled. 'Is Mum all right do you think?' she asked.

'Your mum is a tower of strength,' Nev replied. 'But even she is a bit, well, a bit *down in the dumps* just at the moment.'

'Do you think our petition will work?' Honeysuckle asked anxiously.

'Ducky, if it doesn't work, young, handsome Nev here will go in person and *prostrate* himself in front of the man from the Waterways and *beg* him not to raise the rent!' The others laughed and Honeysuckle did her best to laugh too. Nev continued, 'But what I wanted to say was that you must get yourselves down to the town hall right away! One of my ladies told me that the mayor is there this afternoon and that this would be the absolutely *best* time to go!'

'Rock on!' said Billy. 'Let's hit the road then!'

'I'll leave you to it,' Nev said. 'I've got a blue rinse and a semi-perm coming in at any minute. Bye, duckies – very best of luck!' he said, and vanished through the back door.

'Right, this is it!' Billy said, picking up his banner and waving it dramatically round the kitchen.

'Have we got everything?' Jaime asked, and Honeysuckle nodded.

'You don't think we'll be arrested, do you?' Anita asked shakily.

''Course not,' said Billy. 'This is a democracy. We're allowed to protest – we're crusaders. Let's get on with it!'

'I just need to make a quick call and then we can go,' Honeysuckle said.

When she finished her call, Jaime, Anita and Billy got themselves ready to leave. Honeysuckle picked up her placard and, making sure that she had the petition safely tucked under her arm, they set off towards the town hall.

It felt strange hurrying through the familiar blossom-lined streets of their hometown carrying banners and placards. What was stranger still was that quite a few people joined the Dog Walkers when they saw them on their way to the town hall – people who knew Honeysuckle and Rita and who wanted to help; people who thought it was a disgrace that their life on the canal should be put at risk. This cheered Honeysuckle a little and as they got nearer the town hall she felt braver.

When Honeysuckle, Jaime, Billy and Anita arrived at the steps of the grand old building there were about twenty people with them.

Honeysuckle beamed when she saw Mrs Whitely-Grub and Cupid tottering towards the group. 'Thank you so much for coming! I'm so glad you're here!'

'We wouldn't want to miss this for anything!' the elderly lady said. 'I was delighted to get your telephone call!'

She suggested where it would be best for Honeysuckle and the other protestors to position themselves. Then she began chanting, 'Down with mooring rents! Down with mooring rents!' Although her voice was rather faint and wobbly, all the other people in the crowd took up the chant very quickly and the noise began to grow and swell.

Mrs Whitely-Grub had come prepared. She produced

a silver whistle from her handbag and began blowing it loudly in time with the chanting. Honeysuckle was delighted. She jumped up and down with her placard, shouting as loudly as she could.

There was a sudden lull and Mrs Whitely-Grub nudged Honeysuckle. 'Ah ha!' she said with a big smile. 'Just as we hoped – here comes the mayor!'

Sure enough, a figure appeared at the top of the town hall steps. He was tall and plump and wore a smart, dark suit. Around his neck hung the glinting, golden chains of office. 'Hang on,' Honeysuckle thought to herself. 'That looks like the necklace that I saw in the tea-leaves! It must have been a sign to tell me that I was going to see the mayor!' Very secretly, she felt tremendously proud of herself. With a little more practice she was certain that she would always be able to predict the future, just by reading the tea-leaves.

Her fleeting pride gave way to a feeling of panic as the mayor made his way slowly down the steps towards her. What on earth was she supposed to do now?

She need not have worried. Mrs Whitely-Grub stepped forward and in a quite different, booming voice – which Honeysuckle couldn't believe could come out of Cupid's ancient owner – she said, 'Mr

Mayor! We are here to bring you this petition!' The crowd was silent as Mrs Whitely-Grub reached for the petition. Honeysuckle handed it to her and she gave the clipboard to the mayor before continuing. 'The people of this town think that the rise in mooring rents should be rethought! The Patchwork Snail is one of the great attractions of our town and we feel that Mrs Lovelace should be commended for keeping her houseboat looking so beautiful.' The crowd cheered. 'If anything her rent should be lowered, not raised!'

The crowd cheered again as the mayor took the petition. 'The Waterways should be paying *her* to keep The Patchwork Snail afloat!' someone shouted from the back of the group. There was a shout of, 'Hear, hear!' before the mayor turned and, holding the petition tightly in his hand, went back up the steps and into the town hall.

The crowd broke up slowly. Everyone agreed that it had been an excellent protest but Honeysuckle was still worried. 'When do you think we will hear whether we've done any good?' she asked Mrs Whitely-Grub.

'Oh, my dear,' the old lady answered. 'I don't think it will take long – we'll just have to cross our fingers now and wait and see . . .'

Honeysuckle felt quite odd when the protestors had split up and gone their separate ways. It had all been so exciting, collecting names and making placards and banners and chanting and whistling . . . But now – now there was nothing to do but wait. And nobody knew how long the waiting would go on.

Mrs Whitely-Grub could see that Honeysuckle and her friends were at a loose end and that hanging around outside the town hall wasn't going to do anyone any good. 'Would you like to take Cupid for a little late afternoon stroll?' she asked.

'Of course we would,' Honeysuckle replied gratefully. 'Maybe we could go back to the common and see if they are still filming?' she said to the others.

It was agreed that they would return Cupid in a couple of hours.

'Perhaps we'll see Guy Mount again,' Anita sighed, as they waved goodbye to Mrs Whitely-Grub.

'And Suzie will be pleased to see me,' Billy said confidently.

Honeysuckle couldn't help giggling to herself and hoped that Billy wouldn't notice.

'Shall we put all the placards in the recycling dump on the way?' she suggested. 'I feel a bit of a twit carrying this around with me!' She waved her placard through the spring air, hoping, hoping that all their efforts would make a difference.

Chapter Twelve

The Dog Walkers wandered slowly back towards the common with Cupid trotting along beside them. It was a warm afternoon and the breeze smelled of flowers and newly cut grass. Honeysuckle felt as if she was floating – she was light-headed and giddy. Her feet were hardly touching the ground; all the pressure of the last few days had left her feeling light and empty.

She barely noticed when Billy said, 'Blimey!' as he and Anita and Jaime stopped on the edge of the cricket pitch.

She snapped to her senses though when she heard Suzie Storm's voice shouting, 'How do you expect me to work with IDIOTS like these?'

Honeysuckle saw Ms Storm make a sweeping gesture with her arm that included all the techies and most of the rest of the crew as well. 'Everything's wrong. My costume doesn't fit properly, there's mud on my shoes, the leaves keep rustling when I'm trying to deliver my lines AND I've got the wrong colour towels in my trailer – I particularly wanted *white* towels, not *pink* – it's PATHETIC!'

Billy looked horrified. There was his favourite TV star behaving like a spoiled child. It was really embarrassing.

'I don't think I want to be a TV star if lots of people behave like that,' Honeysuckle said.

'Me neither,' agreed Jaime.

'Why don't we take Cupid round behind the trailers to, you know, give him a proper little walk?' Anita suggested. Everyone knew she meant 'to see if Guy Mount's around' but they all agreed that it would be more fun than watching one of their heroes having a tantrum.

They wove their way between the trailers, trying to catch sight of some of the stars they had seen earlier in the day, but no one was around. The only person they did see was Dirk the dog trainer. As soon as Cupid caught sight of him, the little dog began to bark dementedly. Honeysuckle whisked him behind the nearest trailer and said, 'Why does he *do* this whenever he sees that dog trainer?'

'Beats me,' said Billy, who had joined her behind the trailer.

'Cupid doesn't like him at all, does he?' Anita said. 'I'm sure he senses that there is something, you know, *weird* about him.'

'Actually,' Jaime said, 'he's doing something pretty weird now . . .'

'What?' Anita asked, tucking herself in behind Honeysuckle. 'What's he doing?' Honeysuckle had picked Cupid up so that he wouldn't bark and she poked her head out round the corner of the trailer.

Billy leaned out above her. 'He's just training one of the dogs,' he said. 'It's probably something for the film.'

'What – wiggling along on its stomach, grabbing that loop of rope and wiggling back again? What could that have to do with the story?' asked Jaime.

'Yeah, it looks pretty weird to me, too,' said Anita, who had just been brave enough to peek out from behind Honeysuckle. 'In fact, this whole place is giving me the creeps this afternoon. Shall we take Cupid back now?'

The others agreed; they had already been out for over an hour. 'And then on to The Patchwork Snail for some cake and sandwiches!' Honeysuckle said. Because there was nothing the other Dog Walkers liked more than spending time on the Lovelaces' houseboat, they all agreed.

While they stood on Mrs Whitely-Grub's doorstep after dropping Cupid off, the old lady told Honeysuckle that Rita had a surprise for her. Honeysuckle's heart leaped. 'A surprise?' she said. 'How lovely!' Remembering that her mum would be working late again that night she added, 'But I'll have to wait until she gets back from work to find out what it is.'

'I think you might find that your mother is back from work already,' Mrs Whitely-Grub said knowingly. 'Now, let me pay you.' She handed Honeysuckle a good deal of money, much more than Honeysuckle felt she owed, and said, 'Off you go now, and have your surprise!'

As soon as Honeysuckle reached the wall on the other side of the road she could see Rita. She was sitting on the deck of the houseboat, glittering. It looked as if she was wearing her entire collection of necklaces at once and she had her favourite Oxfam diamanté tiara sparkling around her bright orange hair. She was reading the newspaper.

'Hi, Mum!' Honeysuckle called. 'What are you doing home so early?'

'Honeybunch!' Rita squawked. 'I'm so glad you're here

– all of you,' she added as she saw Jaime, Billy and Anita bound down the steps. 'Look at this,' she said, waving the *Evening News* around. 'You brilliant, wonderful, lovely kids!'

Honeysuckle and the others hurtled down the steps and on to the deck of The Patchwork Snail. Rita held the newspaper out so that they could all see. There, right on the front page, was a picture of all of them – Jaime, Anita, Billy and Honeysuckle – with Guy Mount signing her petition! The headline read, *TV Star Backs Houseboat Petition* and then there was a long article about how sad Guy Mount thought it was that a beautiful houseboat should be put at risk by unnecessary rises in mooring rates. Honeysuckle couldn't believe it.

'Oh ho!' said Rita, smiling fit to burst. 'That's not all! When I got back I found Mr William Watson from the Waterways standing right here!' Rita pointed to the canal bank. 'And all because of you, my brilliant girly and your lovely friends, something stupendously, fabulously, fantastically, wonderfully amazing has happened!' She wrapped her arms round Honeysuckle. 'You won't believe it!' Rita continued, rocking Honeysuckle backwards and forwards.

'What is it?' Honeysuckle's muffled voice came out

from inside Rita's hug. Rita unlocked her arms and held Honeysuckle by the shoulders.

'Your petition!' she shrieked. 'Your petition has been a stonking great success!'

'What, already?' Honeysuckle gasped.

'Absolutely,' said Rita. 'It seems that all the right people were at the town hall today and your petition was discussed and sorted out straight away! Old William Watson esquire, who actually turned out to be quite a sweetie, came to tell me that instead of putting the rent *up* for the mooring, he is putting it *down*! What do you think of that?'

'Wow!' was all Honeysuckle could say; she was so thrilled. She and Rita began jiggling around the deck singing 'We Are The Champions' at the top of their voices. Billy and Jaime and Anita joined in and pretty soon The Patchwork Snail was rocking and bopping on the water like a fairground bouncy castle.

Chapter Thirteen

'Way-hey!' Rita shouted. 'Maybe we'd better stop – don't want to sink this old sieve now that we can actually afford to stay here!' She stood, gasping for breath for a moment. 'I think we should put up all the decorations, don't you, Honeybunch? Before we have a slap-up tea? What do you say?' Honeysuckle couldn't answer before Rita had jumped off the boat and flung open the door of the little blue hut. She pulled out a huge bunch of twizzly multi-coloured windmills. 'Stick these in around the edge of the deck,' she shouted, throwing the bunch of them to Billy. 'Oh and Honeybunch, let's hang up some of these Japanese paper lanterns. You'll have to find some string and thread them across the deck.'

'OK,' said Honeysuckle, pulling the concertina paper

lanterns out to their full size.

Jaime and Anita rushed off shouting, 'We'll be back in a minute – just going to get something!'

They reappeared a little later with an armful of fresh, buttery yellow daffodils. 'They're from my mum's garden,' Jaime explained. 'I know she would want you to have them, to say congratulations!'

'Blooming heck!' said Rita. 'I think I'm going to cry!' She wiped a silvery tear from the corner of her eye and gave them both a huge kiss. 'Let's put the flowers in this painted bucket and stick it on the roof, in amongst the butterflies . . . There!'

Rita stood with her hands on her hips surveying her masterpiece. Honeysuckle and the others jumped off the boat and joined her on the bank. 'Oh!' Anita sighed. 'I don't think I've ever seen anything so, so . . .'

'Abso-blooming-lutely gorgeous!' said Rita, finishing her sentence triumphantly. The Patchwork Snail glowed in the sunlight. There were the huge red and yellow poppies painted all over the roof and the dazzling multi-coloured butterflies, like the patterns in a kaleidoscope, flitting in between the flowers. There was the wobbly striped deck with its tiger-print cushions and the gold swirls that Rita had swished into every tiny empty space.

The whole boat looked magical. Honeysuckle grinned – she loved her home, every single tiny bit of it.

'There's just one more thing I've got to do,' Rita said. 'Poor Mr Gnome here looks so dreary.' She picked up the garden gnome and gave it a smacking kiss. 'We can't have that now, can we, Mr Gnome? I tell you what, why don't you lot go and get the cake, sandwiches and pop organised while I give my little friend here a lick of paint?'

Honeysuckle, Jaime, Billy and Anita squeezed themselves into the galley kitchen and began sorting out the tea things while Rita carefully painted the gnome's hat a brilliant, glossy, lipstick red.

The sunlight made Rita's hair glow like the embers of a fire and her pink and purple spotted pedal-pushers set the red of her little fitted jacket off beautifully. Her necklaces and tiara flashed in the sunlight, glittering as much as the gold of her dancing shoes.

Honeysuckle heard a man's voice coming from the side of the boat. The voice said, 'I don't believe it! Don't move!'

From where they were squeezed in the galley kitchen, Honeysuckle and the others couldn't see the owner of the voice, but it sounded familiar. Honeysuckle saw her mum disobey the voice and turn towards the canal path.

'This is the most perfect sight that I have seen in the last twenty-five years!' the voice went on. Honeysuckle suddenly realised who was speaking and nudged Billy to keep quiet while they waited to see what would happen next. 'My dear lady, would you and your devastating houseboat consider a cameo role in my latest TV show?'

Anita gasped and clapped her hand over her mouth as she too recognised the voice.

'Er . . . um . . .' For once Rita was lost for words.

'Madam, I'm so sorry,' the man's voice continued. 'Let me introduce myself. I'm Greg Gregson, film director and impresario . . .' The Dog Walkers grinned at each other. 'I came to see how your daughter got on with her petition – but now that I see you . . . ! Let me explain. I'm making a little TV show on the common at the moment and what it really needs is a glorious splash of colour and character – just like the vision I see before me now!'

'Oh,' said Rita. 'Pinch me someone, I think I might be dreaming!'

'The dream is all mine, dear lady,' Greg Gregson went on. 'With your permission I will bring my camera crew down to the canal bank and shoot a few minutes of film. What do you think? We could give you a few words to say, nothing too taxing . . .'

'Jumping jellyfish,' Rita said under her breath. 'Are you for real?'

Honeysuckle climbed up on to the deck and smiled at the director. He grinned back at her. 'And this, I know, is your lovely daughter! Not that you look old enough!'

'He's certainly got all the blarney,' Rita whispered to Honeysuckle before saying out loud, 'I dare say I could manage to fit a small TV role into my busy schedule! When were you thinking of doing this filming?'

'You call the shots, dear lady. All I want is for you to be yourself and we'll do the rest – including writing your pay cheque.'

Honeysuckle was afraid her mum might burst with excitement after Greg Gregson had left, but instead of bursting she put her arms round Honeysuckle and said, 'So, we're ALL going to be in the film! How blinking beautiful is that?'

Honeysuckle just smiled.

'I tell you what babes,' her mum said. 'Why don't you go and ask Mrs Whitely-Grub to join in the celebrations? After all, she did so much to help, didn't she? Go on . . .'

Honeysuckle did as her mum asked and Mrs Whitely-Grub tottered down with Honeysuckle on to the boat. They ate cake and sandwiches and danced on the deck and round Rita's tiny garden to Abba. Even Mrs Whitely-Grub managed a little shimmy in the last of the evening sun.

They told stories and Billy recited some of his favourite jokes, most of which made him laugh so much he couldn't always get the punch line out. This in turn made the others giggle hopelessly and Mrs Whitely-Grub had to ask for a tissue to wipe the tears of laughter from her eyes.

Later, they sang pop songs by the light of the moon, with Billy singing the harmonies, sort of. And much, much later when everyone had left and Honeysuckle and Rita had tidied up the last of the cake crumbs, Honeysuckle made herself a cup of tea before getting ready for bed. Rita was undressing in her cabin, which gave Honeysuckle a few moments to check the signs in the tea-leaves. She knew that she hardly needed to – now that her crusade had been such a success – but even so, she thought she would just have a little look. She swirled the remains of the tea around and tipped the cup up on to its saucer. She peered into the bottom of the cup and was very, very surprised to see almost exactly the same shape as she had seen before. 'The mayor's necklace!' she whispered. 'It looks just like the mayor's chain again. Why would I see that now, when I have already seen the mayor today?' As she couldn't think of any answers, Honeysuckle had to go to sleep that night with the question still going round in her head.

Chapter Fourteen

Rita hardly slept that night – her mind was stuffed full of all the wonderful things that had happened during the day. Not only could she afford to stay on The Patchwork Snail, now she and the houseboat were going to be on TV as well!

Honeysuckle buried her head further under her lacy covers when she heard her mum singing in the world's smallest bathroom on Saturday morning. Surely it was too early to be awake? She pulled a corner of the cover down and opened one eye. It was still dark! What on earth was her mum doing?

'Dancing in the dark, la la la la la, dancing in the dark . . .' Rita sang along to the radio. Honeysuckle smiled; it was so great to hear her mum being happy that she could almost forgive her for waking her up too early. She pulled the bedclothes down properly and opened her other eye. All right, she thought, there is a trace of daylight so I suppose I could get up and make Mum some coffee. I'm never going to get back to sleep now anyway with her squeaking away next door.

Honeysuckle climbed out of her bunk, pulling her bedspread round her shoulders before pushing her feet into the warm fluffiness of her slippers.

The kettle was already boiling by the time Rita emerged from the bathroom. She was pink and damp and wrapped in an orange towel. On her feet she wore her golden dancing shoes. 'Honeybunch!' she squealed. 'Top of the morning to you!' She swooped over to Honeysuckle and gave her a toothpastey kiss. 'Such a beautiful morning,' she trilled.

'How can you tell?' Honeysuckle asked, grinning. 'It isn't even properly light yet!'

'Babes – I'm sorry, I couldn't stay in bed another minute – I just feel so excited!' she said, doing a little shimmy in the middle of the saloon.

'Because you're going to be a TV star?' asked Honeysuckle.

'Most of all because we can stay on this floating disaster, but yes, of course – I'm thrilled skinny to think that I'm going to be on the telly . . . I feel like a star already!'

'Is that why you've been wearing your tiara in the bath?' Honeysuckle asked innocently.

'Oh, Honeybunch!' Rita laughed. 'You know somehow I just felt it was the right thing to put on this morning – a bit of glitter, you know?'

Honeysuckle handed her mum a pink mug full of fresh coffee and as Rita got dressed in her own cabin, Honeysuckle made her practise saying things like a film star. 'You have to say "daaaaahling" a lot,' she said. 'And when you've got the voice right, you'll have to practise your Red Carpet Walk.'

'Pulsating prawns – I don't think I'll be going down the red carpet just yet, do you?' Rita reappeared, fully dressed, from her cabin. She still wore her tiara and golden shoes and had added a selection of leopard-print, red and turquoise clothes in between. 'What do you think?' she asked, twirling in the tiny saloon.

'Gorgeous. But aren't you going to be a bit early for work?'

'Got loads to do this morning,' Rita replied. 'Bunked off early yesterday, remember? So I ought to get going right away and get all the boring old paperwork done before my first cut and blow dry arrives.' She leaned over and gave Honeysuckle another kiss before picking up her orange shoulder bag and hurtling like a whirlwind up the steps to the hatch. 'We could do a charity shop trawl at the weekend, what do you say?' she called.

'Yeah!' Honeysuckle squeaked in excitement.

'Leave everything shipshape,' Rita shouted, opening the hatch.

'Aye aye, Captain,' Honeysuckle replied as the hatch banged shut and she was on her own.

She turned the light off and snuggled into the corner of the bench with her cup of tea and a piece of jammy toast. She watched the sun make weak streaks of milky light across the canal while the ducks paddled noiselessly along. She listened to the chatter of the early morning radio show as the embers of the previous night's fire glowed in the little stove. The Patchwork Snail gave a friendly creak and rocked peacefully in the water.

Honeysuckle thought about Suzie Storm and her dreadful tantrums. She decided that however famous Rita got, she would never behave like that. She was day-dreaming about how impressed all her friends at school were going to be when a news item on the radio caught her attention.

'. . . Ms Storm is said to be in a state of shock, having discovered in the early hours of this morning that a valuable designer pearl and diamond necklace was missing from the trailer in which she had been sleeping. The local police have not been able to find any clues as to who might have committed this serious crime. They say there are no signs of a break-in. The only possible access into the trailer was through a small open air-vent. No fingerprints have, as yet, been found . . .'

Honeysuckle stared wide-eyed into the brightening morning. 'Of course, that's what the sign in the tea-leaves meant! That's why I saw a necklace, not once but twice! It wasn't anything to do with the mayor. It was a warning that there was going to be a burglary and that a necklace would be stolen! And I bet I know who the thief is!'

She jumped up and was washed and dressed within three minutes. She rushed to the nearest call box and rang Billy, Jaime and Anita. She told them all to meet her as soon as possible on the common. She apologised for ringing so early but explained that there was an emergency.

She raced out of the boat and across the garden. Then, pounding up the steps, she suddenly saw Mrs Whitely-Grub with Cupid. It would have been rude to rush straight past her so she said, 'Good morning!'

'I'm so glad to see you my dear!' Mrs Whitely-Grub beamed. 'What a wonderful evening we had! And, I've just managed to get an early appointment with your mother. It would be marvellous if you could take little Cupie for me this morning, so that I don't have to take him with me . . .' Having a dog with her really was the last thing that Honeysuckle wanted, but she couldn't explain it all to Mrs Whitely-Grub now. The quickest thing to do was to say, 'Yes, of course I will', take the little dog's lead and make a dash for the common.

It was as if Cupid sensed Honeysuckle's urgency. He bounded along so quickly on his spindly little legs that within a few minutes they were both panting at the edge of the common.

'What's up?' asked Billy and Jaime, rushing up to meet her. 'What's the emergency?'

'It's nothing horrible, is it?' Anita asked anxiously as she joined them.

Honeysuckle told them everything: the news about the burglary; the signs in her tea-leaves; and the strange feelings they had all had about a certain person the day before.

'So you think Dirk might have stolen Suzie Storm's necklace?' Anita gulped.

'Not exactly,' said Honeysuckle, 'but don't you see? It all fits! The little air-vent – the fact that there were no *finger*prints . . .'

Anita still looked puzzled.

'You mean you think he got one of his dogs to steal the necklace?' asked Jaime.

'That's it!' Billy wheezed. 'Of course – he said he could get his dogs to do *anything* – he could have got one of them to get through the air-vent and fetch the necklace! That's what he was training his dog to do yesterday!'

'Exactly,' said Honeysuckle.

'So we have to go and find him!' Billy shouted. He turned and started running across the common to the furthest group of trailers. Jaime and Honeysuckle followed with Anita behind them.

'But what will we do when we find him?' she called. Actually, none of the other Dog Walkers had given this much thought.

'I don't believe it!' gasped Billy, coming to a sudden halt. 'Where's his trailer gone?' The others stared in disbelief.

'Maybe he moved it somewhere else close by,' said Honeysuckle, looking round frantically. They searched everywhere but there was no sign of the dog trainer's trailer.

'I'll go and ask the director,' said Jaime. 'Look! I can see him over there.'

The others waited and watched while Jaime talked to Greg Gregson. She ran back shouting, 'He's gone! He went very late last night! Greg says his dogs did their bit of filming, he was paid in cash and then he packed up and left. No one knows where he comes from . . . or even what his surname is.' She looked panic-stricken.

'What are we going to do?' Anita asked.

'We could go to the police,' Billy suggested.

'But we haven't any evidence,' said Jaime. 'And we don't even know his full name. Why would they believe us?'

'I *knew* there was something weird about him,' Anita said. 'Didn't I say yesterday that I thought he was creepy?'

Billy slumped down on the dewy grass and Jaime joined him. Anita went and leaned against the trunk of a nearby tree while Honeysuckle stood holding Cupid and staring into space.

'I think we've blown it,' Jaime said. 'Mind you, she does kind of deserve it!'

'What d'you mean?' Billy asked sharply. 'Who deserves what?'

'Well,' Jaime said slowly, 'you know – Suzie Storm. She is a bit . . .'

'A bit of a spoiled drama queen?' Anita added helpfully.

'Mmm,' Jaime replied. Billy did his best to look disbelieving but even he had to grudgingly agree that Suzie Storm hadn't behaved particularly well on the set.

'Still, I wish we could have found that dog trainer,' Honeysuckle said.

'Wait a minute, wait a minute, WAIT a minute!' The Dog Walkers all turned to see a small man carrying a large megaphone, scuttling across the grass towards them.

'Hello!' he squeaked breathlessly as he got up to where Honeysuckle was standing. 'The director wants to use you and this little dog here for the episode's closing shot! What do you say?'

Chapter Fifteen

It's funny how things don't always work out as you would expect. Honeysuckle knew that if she had been cleverer about the signs in her crystal ball and the messages in the tea-leaves, she might have got more things right. As it was, she and the other Dog Walkers had missed the chance of possibly turning in a real live thief to the police. (Suzie Storm's designer necklace was never found.) She had to learn to trust her instincts, she told herself, and to understand her fortune-telling gift a little better.

Well, she thought, Suzie Storm's necklace and Dirk, the shady dog trainer, might have disappeared but there was still the fact that she and her very best, best friends had managed to stop the mooring rates from rising. In fact, all their efforts had meant the rates went down, which was more than even Honeysuckle could have hoped for. And then there was the TV show, *Inspector Codey*, to look forward to. Not to mention Honeysuckle and Rita's 'starring' roles . . .

Months later, on the evening their episode was to be shown, Rita and Honeysuckle joined the other Dog Walkers at Anita's house, to watch on her wide-screen TV. Honeysuckle felt almost sick with excitement and she could see that Rita was jittery too. She even caught her mum holding her wrist and counting backwards, which meant that she wanted to smoke. She didn't though – Rita hadn't smoked a single cigarette for months now. Billy was making more noise than usual, even though he knew he wouldn't be in the programme. He was doing his best to get everyone over-excited, which really wasn't necessary. He bounded round the room and bounced off the furniture, making gorilla noises. Anita looked wide-eyed and petrified, like a rabbit caught in a car's headlights. Jaime jumped up and down and shouted at Billy to be quiet, but in between she couldn't stop giggling nervously.

Finally it was time for the programme to begin. They snuggled into the depths of the huge soft sofa in Anita's sitting room. While they munched on toffee popcorn, Rita and Honeysuckle, Jaime, Anita and Billy (who didn't want to be left out) waited impatiently for their big moments.

But these too were not quite what they had expected, despite the tea-leaves surely predicting that both Honeysuckle and her mum could look forward to starry futures. Rita's scene was so fleeting that anyone would miss it if they blinked at the wrong moment, which Honeysuckle did. The three girls and their dogs were walking too far in the background to be more than a smudgy blur. And the glorious closing shot of Honeysuckle and Cupid showed nothing more than Cupid and a tiny bit of Honeysuckle's left hand!

'I don't believe it!' Rita squawked. 'That entire hullabaloo and that's all we've got to show for it? What a blooming swizzle!' Then she began to laugh. Her laughter was so infectious that the others laughed too. 'I suppose I won't be needing a frock for the Oscars then?' Rita wheezed, wiping her eyes. She stood up and pretended to pose for photographers. 'I just want to thank my agent,' she said between hiccups. 'And my neighbour's poodle,' she snorted. 'And the duck by my houseboat . . .'

As the credits rolled, Rita and the Dog Walkers all roared with laughter before deciding that, quite honestly, the show had been a terrible letdown. Being a TV star was definitely not all it was made out to be.

When they wandered out of Anita's house and into the street, Rita and Honeysuckle found, unsurprisingly, that there were no fans waiting to mob them. Indeed, no one greeted the little group as they strolled, arm in arm, slowly back through the leafy streets of the town. Billy and Jaime said their goodbyes and left Rita and Honeysuckle to make their way back to the canal. In a few minutes, they would be able to see their spectacular floating work of art – the only home Honeysuckle Sabrina Florette Lovelace had ever known.

Rita put her arm round Honeysuckle's shoulders and gave her a little squeeze as The Patchwork Snail came into view. 'You see, Honeybunch, we shouldn't be disappointed. I mean, why would we need to be TV stars when you and I are already Princesses of The Patchwork Snail?'

'You know something, Mum?' said Honeysuckle, laughing. 'You are absolutely, completely and positively right!'

Cherry
Whytock

Honeysuckle
Lovelace

The Dog Walkers' Club

There comes a time in almost everybody's life when
they have a brilliant idea. Honeysuckle Lovelace's
Brilliant Idea is to set up a Dog Walkers' Club with
her friends. She can spend time with her favourite
animals *and* earn some money to help mend the leaky
houseboat where she and her mum live.

The club's first 'client' is Cupid, Mrs Whitely-Grub's
pinky-white poodle, who barely even passes for a dog.
As Cupid becomes a regular client, Honeysuckle is
increasingly suspicious of his owner. She's determined
to solve the mysteries surrounding Mrs Whitely-Grub
– and the Dog Walkers' Club provides the perfect cover!

Cherry
Whytock

Honeysuckle Lovelace

Ghosthunters

The Dog Walkers' Club is going from strength to strength. Honeysuckle and her friends already have plenty of clients and they've just got another one: a twitchy whippet called Twitter.

Life at home with her mum is not going so well. Honeysuckle is not at all keen on Rita's idea to move from the leaky houseboat, or on her new admirer – who keeps scaring them with spooky local stories.

When Twitter's owner asks Honeysuckle to dog-sit in her old, creaky house, Honeysuckle remembers one of the spooky stories. After a deeply scary time there, she wonders if the house is haunted . . .

Other Piccadilly Pearls

Girl Writer

Ros Asquith

Features top writing tips for aspiring authors!

Castles and Catastrophes

Cordelia Arbuthnott wants to write books. Not the sort that her aunt, the bestselling children's author Laura Hunt writes, but literary masterpieces. A writing competition at her dreaded new school seems just the opportunity, but writing a masterpiece is trickier than she expected; real life just keeps getting in the way.

Sleuths and Truths

Cordelia loves to read about Sherlock Holmes and now writes stories about his younger sister, Charlotte. But then Cordelia discovers a real life mystery to solve – she is convinced a man has been wrongly convicted. But is she right?

ECO-WORRIERS

Kathryn Lamb

Penguin Problems

Committed eco-worriers, Evie and Lola, are very, very concerned about green issues – much to the irritation of their gas-guzzling families!

So when they find a penguin chick in the garden they're really worried. Have the ice caps finally melted and the poor penguins been forced into new lands?

It turns out that this particular penguin was taken from the local wildlife park. Could the penguin-napping be linked to the awful, but completely unfounded, rumours circulating about the park? Lola and Evie are determined to investigate further, and the more they find out the more suspicious they become . . .

SeaGirls

g.g. elliot

The Crystal City

Finding out that she can breathe underwater is only the beginning of Polly's discoveries.

Even before this, she's always felt different. But then she finds a kindred spirit in Lisa. The two girls discover that they both have the same fish-shaped birthmark, were both adopted, and can both breathe underwater. Surely it can't just be coincidence?

When a strong current drags them to the depths of the ocean, they not only discover their true identities, but an amazing world – more incredible and more disturbing than they could ever have imagined . . .

JONNY ZUCKER

Stunt★Girl

Venus Spring is fourteen and this is the first summer she's been allowed to go to stunt camp. It is a dream come true – something she has been working towards for years. But while she is there, she stumbles on a devious and terrifying plot that threatens the surrounding countryside, and Venus is determined to uncover it.

Body★Double

When DCI Radcliff hears a rumour that a gang intends to kidnap teen movie star Tatiana Fairfleet, she asks Venus to act as Tatiana's body double at her boarding school – providing a decoy if there are any problems. But Venus soon finds herself in real danger, and needs to rely on all her stunt skills to stop events spiralling out of control.

☆

www.piccadillypress.co.uk

☆ The latest news on forthcoming books

☆ Chapter previews

☆ Author biographies

☆ Fun quizzes

☆ Reader reviews

☆ Competitions and fab prizes

☆ Book features and cool downloads

☆ And much, much more . . .

Log on and check it out!

Piccadilly Press